The Valley of Dying Stars

A Mark Christian Detective Novel

By

J.D. Miller

ISBN: 1-4107-0862-4 (e-book)
ISBN: 1-4107-0863-2 (Softcover)

This book is printed on acid free paper.

1stBooks - rev. 03/29/03

ACKNOWLEDGEMENTS

Thanks to my editor Carol, wife Diane, and good friend Terrey for their invaluable feedback, encouragement, and editing suggestions.

Thanks to Scott, Uncle Ferdi, Ruth, my sister Paula and parents Jim and Anna for encouraging me to write, and to my wife Diane and son Jonathan, who never complained during the many hours I spent immersed in this project. Without such a supportive family, this would have been much more difficult, if not impossible.

Thanks to Bruce and Kerrey for the guidance on marketing and promotion.

And, of course, special thanks to Greg for paving the way. No one could ask for a more supportive friend. Without you none of this would have happened.

The author can be contacted at

Markcmystery@aol.com

Lovingly dedicated to my son, Jonathan.

There are no eyes here

In this valley of dying stars

In this hollow valley

This broken jaw of our lost kingdoms.

- T.S. Elliot

-1-

The hand holding the .38 shifted slightly, pressing the cold steel of the barrel more firmly into my left temple.

It's amazing the clarity of perception you get at moments like this. As the gun moved I could feel the curved striations of the inner barrel slightly scratching against my temple and the smooth expanse of its outer surface, warming rapidly as it took the heat from my flesh, as if it is already drawing the life from me. I can hear the soft song of a bird perched outside the window, the low hum of the air conditioner, and the soft rhythmic panting of Rachel, the world's *worst* watchdog. If I made it through this I'd have to give her a class in doggy basics. Rule One: When someone is holding a gun to your masters head, *attack!* Don't lie under the kitchen table, watching curiously.

So this is it, I thought, disappointed that my life was not flashing before my eyes. It would have been pretty interesting. I'd especially like to relive that night with Susie Johnson when I was seventeen. That was amazing! The things that girl could do with her…well, never mind…if I am going to heaven soon, thoughts of sex probably won't help with my chances for admission. Better think of something profound: Recite the twenty-third psalm or something.

I'm surprised I'm not feeling more panicked about this. Don't get me wrong; I'm concerned, but not on the level that one would expect. Maybe it has something to do with the large dose of Percocet I took in the car on the way here. And where is here? What journey led me to this point? That will take a lot of explaining...

3 months earlier

Old Town Warrenton, Virginia

I was sitting in my office smoking about the tenth Salem of the day when she walked in. Old, slightly stooped, skin the color of worn leather. She sat down in the chair across from my desk and hacked softly at the cloud of smoke that hung in the room.

Her face screwed up slightly in distaste as she said "You don't look like no private eye to me."

"What does a private eye look like?"

"Older I suppose...like on TV."

"I'm older than I look."

"Hmph," she said as she scanned me steadily, trying to figure out if I knew what I was doing. "Well, you definitely got the build for it."

"Thanks. So what can I do for you ma'am?" I asked, hoping to move things along.

"My name's Lillian Jones. I need some help, but I ain't got much extra money right now. When I told the sheriff that, they sent me to you."

I tried not to blush at this latest round of flattery. "That'd be Tom Harris," I said, almost to myself.

"Yes," she said, looking mildly surprised. "Deputy Harris. He said you might be willing to take on someone that can't pay much. And sho' nuff I can't pay much of nothin', " she said, shaking her head for emphasis. "How you know him?"

2

"We met on a previous case, kept in touch afterwards, and became friends. He's the only person in the Sheriff's Office who would know that I'm fiscally challenged," I said wryly. She was looking at me blankly so I elaborated. "Who would know that I'm currently low on cash, and therefore, willing to take on clients who can't pay much."

"Oh. He also told me that you wasn't one of them private eyes who go slinkin' around outside of motels, tryin' to catch someone cheatin'. He said that people hire you for the rough stuff."

"That's true. I also do some executive protection on occasion."

We sat quietly for a moment. I took a drag on my cigarette and blew the smoke towards the slice of sky in the open window.

"You read all these books?" she asked, gesturing vaguely towards the bookshelves that lined the walls.

"Yes."

"You ain't no intellectual, is you?"

"No. I just like to read."

"Good. Never did meet an intellectual that could get a damn thing done."

I smiled and said, "Me neither. Not anyone that was just an intellectual, anyways."

"So what else you do besides read?"

I didn't like answering these questions from a stranger, but felt like I ought to be patient with them. This was basically my profession's equivalent of a job interview.

"Well, before I got into this, I spent some time in the Marines."

"Really," she said, pleased now. "My other son is an officer in the army. He fought over there in Iraq. Now he teaches at West Point."

"I did some time in Iraq and Mogadishu,." I added while taking another drag on my cigarette.

"You grow up around here?"

"No. I was born in Northwestern Pennsylvania, near Erie. My parents were killed in a car crash. I lived a while with an uncle and his family, but that didn't work out too well. I eventually went to live in a catholic seminary up there."

"Oh? How come it didn't work out at your uncle's?"

"He had an alcohol problem," I said, surprised at the effort of will it took to keep the hostility out of my voice.

She raised her eyebrows, having caught my tone of forced casualness. She wisely decided to let it go. "So if you was in the seminary," she said, "how come you didn't become a priest?"

"For a while I thought I would. But as I got older, I found that there were some things about the church that I couldn't agree with, so I moved on. I'm grateful to them though; the seminary provided me with a family I wouldn't have had otherwise."

There was another silence during which she gave me one last searching look and then seemed to come to a decision.

"My son Eric was killed six months ago. Shot dead two blocks from his home in Northeast Washington, DC. As usual, the police ain't found shit. I want you to find whoever did this and put 'em in jail," she said.

"Forgive me for asking, but was he in the life?"

"No! He was a nice boy! Didn't ever get into trouble. Worked at the government printing office and went to church regular and all that. Never knew him to bother no one."

"So why would someone want to kill him?" I asked.

"The police told us they think it was a case of mistaken identity. That whoever done this was actually gunnin' for some drug dealer and mistook Eric for that person in the dark."

"If that's true, it'll make it tough to find out who did it. Most murders are committed by someone who knows the victim. If there is no connection, like in a contract killing, it becomes especially hard to solve."

"Are you saying you can't do it?" she asked, her tone abrupt.

"Ms. Jones, I'm no salesman. I'm too inclined to tell the hard truth, and let the chips fall where they may. So here it is: it will be difficult, and I can't guarantee I can find out who did it, and I will still expect to be paid for the time I spend even if I can't."

"So why should I hire you? What can you do that the cops haven't already done?"

"I can work on the case full time. Many homicide detectives are overwhelmed with an enormous number of cases, especially in a city like DC. So their attention is divided, they make mistakes, miss connections, and do a less than thorough job. A lot of them are burned out, too, and they tend to ignore cases that are not easily solved. Most murder cases are solved within the first forty-eight hours, and in more difficult cases it can be hard to find the motivation to keep working. Also, not being a part of the police bureaucracy, I can get things done quicker. I don't have to fill out 20 forms every time I do something, or ask for approval."

She paused for a long moment, searching my face with the sharpness of someone good at sizing people up. Then she took a deep breath, nodded slowly, and said, "Ok," and I knew I was hired.

Lillian Jones stayed another few minutes as we discussed various practicalities; names and addresses of people I would need to interview, costs, etc. Then I held the door for her as she walked out with the slow, gingerly gait of the aged.

-2-

I'd decided long ago that a safe life is not worth living. Hence, my choice of transportation, a beat-up old Triumph motorcycle. I opened her up going west down 211, heading home through the foothills of the Shenandoah, relishing the warm wind on my face. It was the first real day of spring with the sky a rich, cloudless baby-blue and a clean, warm breeze that gently rustled the leaves.

I slowed down and cornered onto a one-lane country road and within minutes entered a majestic valley in the heart of the Blue Ridge Mountains. The road was bordered intermittently by Civil-War-style stone fences and rolling meadows, filled with yellow flowers and grazing horses.

Eventually I took a left onto a dirt road that headed up a mountain. My home was far up, near to heaven. It sat on a break in the carpet of oak and pine that covered the mountain. It was a small, worn clapboard house dating from the early 1900's. Its best feature—besides the cost—was the sagging wraparound porch with its spectacular view of the valley below and surrounding mountains. After living in the city for a couple of years, I had discovered it on a weekend trip and knew instantly I that had found my place in the world.

I killed the engine on the Triumph and hopped off. Rachel, my SPCA-bought mutt, came tearing out of the woods and pounced on me. She was half-collie and half- black lab, and the prodigious fur around her head and neck tickled as she gave me a sloppy tongue-

7

J.D. Miller

lashing. I rubbed her tummy and soothed her with some baby talk, then went into the house. She trotted after me contentedly.

After changing clothes, I went outside and started my hour workout. I had a regular routine, done every third day. It consisted of endless sets of pushups, sit-ups, squats, leg lifts, and pull-ups hanging off the thick branch of a oak tree, with two twenty-five pound weights tied to my waist by a special belt. Moderation had never been one of my virtues, and my workouts were no exception.

Rachel also had a routine during my workouts. First, she curled up in the shade of a tree and watched me curiously for a minute, probably wondering why I was bouncing up and down for no apparent reason. Then she drifted off into a brief nap.

I was about a half hour into it when a voice sang out from downhill, "Mark!"

Rachel jumped up and charged into the woods after the voice, tail wagging furiously. A minute or two later she returned, tail still wagging, followed by Alicia Hunsaker, my neighbor's daughter. The Hunsaker's lived at the base of the mountain, and had become friends. Alicia was an only child, fifteen, skinny, and angular. Her long blond hair shimmered in the sunlight. I was her first crush, and a young girl's heart can be a fragile thing, so I hid my irritation at having my workout interrupted.

"Hi," I panted as I finished up a set of pushups.

"Hi," she said brightly, sitting down in the grass cross-legged. Rachel curled up next to her, and Alicia petted her absentmindedly. "How many of those do you do, anyway?"

"About four hundred and fifty of each exercise, in sets of one-fifty."

"How do you do that many?" she asked, eyes wide.

"It took about three years to work up to those numbers. When I started, I could only do fifty comfortably. I kept at it, adding about ten reps per month until I got to where I am today. Goes to show you," I said, resting between sets, "you can do anything if you stick with it long enough. Even if you improve slowly, all those little improvements can add up to something big over time."

"Wow," was her only response, as she scratched Rachel behind the ears.

What I didn't tell her—I didn't have the energy to explain it past the blank looks I usually got from people—was that it was one of the many ways that I sought the purity on the other side of suffering. I didn't work out for the same reasons as most people. For me, it was not about losing weight or having killer abs or pecs; it was about developing inner strength, peace and clarity. It is an emotional cleansing. And, of course, there were professional reasons.

"Where's Pete?" I asked after a set of pull-ups. Pete was one of two horses the Hunsakers owned and Alicia's favorite. She usually rode him when she came to visit. "Is he ok?"

"Yes," she said. "He's a little moody today, didn't want to take the saddle, so I left him."

I finished up and lay in the grass a few minutes, dripping sweat and relishing the after-workout high. Eventually I sat up and said, "It looks like I may have to go into the city for a few days. Can you take care of Rachel for me?"

"Sure, she comes down the mountain a couple times a day, anyway. We'll put some food out and let her come in the house whenever she wants."

"Thanks. You're a sweetheart."

She blushed.

Some time later Alicia went home, not wanting to be late for dinner.

I went inside, took a shower, then spent the rest of the day on the front porch in an old rocker, nursing a beer and reading Mushima's *Sun and Steel*.

The next morning I had a quick breakfast and then dressed in a light navy shirt, khaki pants, and my favorite leather motorcycle boots. I went to the dresser and took out an M-1911A1 .45 automatic that I had "borrowed" from the Marine Corps. In the age of the 9mm, I still swore by the .45. It's dependable and has serious stopping power. Its heavy 230-grain bullet will knock a man down with the first round so he won't get back up. Plus the .45 ACP slug travels relatively slowly, so it's less likely to go through the target, reducing the chances of hitting a bystander.

When I had been in the Marine Corps, I'd had it accurized by one of the best gunsmiths in the country. He'd worked the slide, barrel, barrel bushing, and receiver until they were smooth and given me a National Match trigger, adjusted to my grip. The Bo Mar sight was removed and replaced by a special rear-set sight.

I checked the load and safety, put it in my shoulder holster, grabbed a leather jacket and helmet, then jumped on my Triumph and started the two-hour trip into Washington, DC.

The first leg took me down Route 211 through the emerald hills of the Shenandoah. At Warrenton I took a left onto 29. It was a pleasant trip with a clean warm wind, cloudless blue skies, and little traffic until I drove east on 66.

Closer to the city, the traffic arteries thickened and the drivers became more rushed and inpatient. At one point I found myself racing beside a silver Metrotrain that ran next to the road, its riders staring absently out the window or reading the paper. Planes began to soar past on their departure route from National Airport.

Finally I flew over the Memorial bridge into the city, down Constitution Avenue and onto H street. Mid-way down H street, I passed Union Station and the invisible demarcation between the white and black sections of the city.

I had arrived in one of the worst neighborhoods in Southeast Washington. This was not the Washington of the Monuments and Mall, White House and Supreme Court. It was not the part of the city that you see on the national news as backdrop for the talking heads. This was 'Southeast,' decimated by poverty and drug use, known as the "murder capitol of the world," where four to five homicides a night were considered routine, and the police only solved less than half of the cases. Small children often slept on the floor at night to reduce the chances of being hit by a stray round coming through a window. There had been stories of crack-addicted moms, in order to get money for drugs, forcing their pre-teen daughters to prostitute themselves, of wide-spread police corruption, and of eight-year-old children working as lookouts for drug dealers. Infant mortality rates matched those of the

J.D. Miller

worst Third-World countries, and almost two-thirds of the adult males had criminal records.

I parked my Triumph on H Street in front of the local police station. It was located in a small dirty shopping center, wedged between a McDonalds and a boarded up store. The door was locked, and I was let in only after identifying myself to the desk sergeant over an intercom. Not a bad idea in a neighborhood where shooting at the police is considered a right of passage.

I walked in, checked my .45 at the desk, and sat down to wait to talk to someone. The station was small, basically one room with a few desks, bathed in fluorescent light. Other than the desk sergeant, there was only one other cop here, busy typing some report while talking on the phone.

After twenty minutes of waiting, a large man with a hard face, wearing a ratty shirt and tie, came out of an office in the back and waved me over. When I entered, he said, "I'm Lt. Weldon. How can I help you."

"Mark Christian," I said as we shook hands. I sat down in the chair across from his desk. "I'm a private investigator."

"Can I see your license?"

I handed it over. He scrutinized it carefully and then handed it back, saying, "Bad picture."

"Thanks."

"So what do you want?"

"I've been hired by a woman named Lillian Jones to investigate the murder of her son Eric. She said your station was the one that looked into the murder originally. I wondered if you had any information I could use."

12

"Hold on. Let me get the file." He leaned over and started thumbing through a cabinet drawer, saying "I need it to refresh my memory. We get at least one murder a night in this precinct...Hold up. Here it is."

He pulled the file out with a yank and placed it on his desk, and then quickly browsed the pages. Then he handed it to me and said, "O.k. My memory is refreshed. Shoot."

As I flipped through the file, I asked "What happened?"

"Guy was walking home from work late one night and got taken out in a drive-by. They fucked up his day real good; hit him twice in the stomach with an automatic shotgun. Almost blew him in half."

"I see that," I said. I was looking at one of the crime scene pictures. Eric lay on his back in front of a decrepit rowhouse, staring blankly at the night sky, his upper and lower bodies barely connected by a strip of exposed muscle on his left side. Everything else was spread out around him. "Hit him twice in the same place from a moving vehicle. Good shot."

"More likely a lucky shot," the Lieutenant said absently, leaning back in his chair. "The local boys aren't to well known for their marksmanship. I've seen guys unload a whole clip at someone 20 yards away and miss with every shot."

"So why do you think it's a case of mistaken identity?"

"Seemed like the most likely explanation. We looked into the victim's background; he was as clean as a whistle. No prior arrests, just a couple of traffic tickets. No known enemies, no drug use, very little money. What I'm saying is that we couldn't find any reason why someone would want to kill this guy. Mistaken identity seemed like the best explanation. He was killed a few yards away from a known drug corner while he walked home from work. They probably mistook him for one of the corner dealers and aced him."

"Wearing a nice shirt and tie on a well-lit street?"

"Stranger things have happened. You think all the dealers in D.C. wear Timberlands and gold chains? Some of them are working stiffs, who sling dope in the evening to supplement their salary."

"Hmmm. What else have you got?"

"One reluctant witness, who saw a gold Lexus. Didn't get a license."

"Any leads?"

"Not any we could prove," he said.

"How about some you can't prove."

"Not really."

"Good to know you guys are on the case."

"Is that supposed to be smart?"

"Sarcastic, actually."

"Get the fuck out of my office."

"Yeah, thanks for the help," I said, and walked out.

-3-

After that little rapport-building session with the local police, I drove ten blocks north to my next interview.

"Pat! There's some white man here! Says he wants to see you!"

I was standing in front of an immaculate row house on Sixth Street northeast. The yard was carefully tended and a bank of flowers lined the porch. It was a showpiece compared to the other houses on the street, most of which hadn't seen a paint job in decades. A couple of them looked ready to collapse.

The voice belonged to a pretty young girl of about fifteen, eyeing me suspiciously through the screen door.

"Mind your manners!" a voice yelled from somewhere in the house. "That's Mr. Christian that called earlier. Let him in."

The girl led me through the house to the kitchen. We found Ms. Pat Jones hunched over the sink washing dishes, bathed in the whitish-yellow light coming in through a window. Late fifties, with an air of strength and hard-won dignity. I liked her immediately. She turned off the tap, dried her hands, and we exchanged greetings. I accepted an offer of coffee and a seat at the kitchen table.

The girl said, "Can I go upstairs?"

"Sure, hon. We don't need you for this."

The girl gave me a final appraising glance and then shot out of the kitchen. A moment later I heard her galumphing up the stairs.

"That's my God-daughter. I watch her while her mom's at work."

"Oh. Thanks for seeing me," I said. "As I mentioned over the phone, I'm investigating Eric's death. Lillian told me yesterday that you're her sister, and Eric's aunt."

"Yes. Awful what happened to that boy."

I murmured some condolences, which she seemed to accept, and then asked "Tell me a little about Eric; what kind of man was he?"

"He was a good man. I was always proud to have him as a nephew. Deacon in our church. When everybody else was leaving the city, he stayed. I remember him saying that if all the good people left, there really was no hope for the children still here. He used to say all the time that "if you never see positive, how can you ever learn to do positive?"

"Sounds like a saint," I said between sips of coffee.

"Well, he wasn't no saint. But he was a *real* good man. We had some trouble with him as a teenager; it's especially easy to lose them to the streets at that age. Eric muddled through and straightened out when he got to Howard University."

"Did he have any arguments with anyone just before he died? Make any enemies, break up with a girlfriend? Anything that might explain why this happened?"

"Nothing I know of," she said. "Except the fact that he was born black and in this city."

There was a brief silence as her words hung in the air. I sipped my coffee, then asked "What did Eric do for a living?"

"He was a supervisor at the government print shop over on K street. He used to walk home from work every night. That always made me nervous. He walked home in his nice professional clothes and leather briefcase and that made him stand out. I was always worried that some dope fiend would kill him, thinking he had some money for drugs."

"Is that what you think happened?"

"No," she said forcefully. "Ain't a dope fiend alive that carries a shotgun. Any dope fiend that got money for a gun is dealin'. And anyone dealin' don't need to rob no one for a billy. The only thing they rob is their own supply. A dope fiend is going to rob you with a piece of glass he picked up off the street or an ice pick he stole from his mother."

"Sounds like you speak from experience."

"Almost fifty years in a neighborhood will teach you a few things. I been mugged four times in my life," she said disgustedly. "Them drugs, they are truly of the devil. This used to be a nice city back in the day. Me and my sister—when we was yung 'uns—used to go dancing at the local swing club and walk home at dark and never worried a bit. The streets was clean, and people looked out for one another. Then around '65, the drugs started coming in and it all started to go to hell. Mothers and fathers walked out on their families to run the streets, people stopped working, and it got so you had to watch your back all the time."

She paused and briefly scanned my face. Seeing interest there, she continued.

"Just when we all thought it couldn't get any worse, crack came along and took it to a whole new level. Blood ran in the streets, for real. Almost every day you heard about someone you knew getting shot or going to jail. A lot of people turned to drugs during that time just to relieve the pressure of living in all of that. You ever been around here on New Years Eve?"

"Yes," I answered. "I lived in Northwest off Columbia Road for a couple of years. I was down here one New Years Eve, working a case. It seemed like everyone in the city was shooting guns into the air to celebrate. It was like Dodge City. I didn't hear that much gunfire in Iraq."

"Then you know a little bit about it. That's good. I was afraid you was some white guy who didn't know what he was getting' into. Especially after Lillian told me you lived out near her in the country."

"I only moved out there last summer. How about Lillian?"

"She moved out after Eric was killed. Swore she'd never live another day in the city. Can't say I blame her."

Shit. An hour of waiting and he still hadn't showed. Endless dragging minutes spent sitting on my motorcycle, sweating in the heat, watching the neighborhood go about it's business, every passerby pretending not to see me but keenly aware of my presence. It was as if every person was silently screaming, "You don't belong here!"

There was something else. It was in the hunch of the shoulders, the quick-darting glances that betrayed a habitual hypervigilance. It confirmed for me how dangerous this place could be, how anything could happen to anyone at anytime.

My eyes scanned the place for the thousandth time. I was on Eleventh street, about twenty yards north of its intersection with H. Parked cars and battered row houses lined the street.. The strips of lawn adjacent the sidewalk were decorated with broken bottles, greasy rags, wrappers, crushed cigarette butts, a dumped box, and a scarred, ripped mattress put out for collection.

In the yard across the street is the place where Eric Jones fell, nearly cut in half. The place where he had spent his last living moments. Had he gazed up into the night sky as the life bled out of him? Had he known who had shot him or gone into the darkness unknowing? The look on his face in the police pictures had been one of shock, which is not necessarily significant. Most people who die of gunshot wounds have a shocked look. Those knifed often have a suprisingly relaxed look.

A police car pulled sharply to the curb and braked hard with a swift screech of tires.

At last. This had to be him: Officer Jeremiah Connel, the first person at the scene the night of Eric Jones' death. I had remembered his name from the file that Lt. Welton had shown me, and tracked him down to arrange this meeting.

He hopped out of the car, a big man with a bulging belly and jet-black skin split by a joyful grin. As he came towards me, he yelled, "Hey," to someone he knew down the street. They turned at his voice and waved back, genuinely smiling, then continued walking.

Officer Connel planted himself a yard away and took me in with a sharp glance. His grin faded.

"You either that private dick I'm supposed to meet, or some dude in town trying to 'cop' drugs. Either way, I'm in the right place."

"What makes you think that I might be copping drugs?" I asked, curious.

"The only two kinds of white people that come down here are social workers and drug addicts; and you don't look like no social worker."

"I'm the private detective, Mark Christian. Thanks for doing this."

"No problem. What do you want to know?"

"Everything you saw at the scene of Eric Jones' murder."

"Why? You already talked to the Lieutenant. He's the lead on the investigation."

"He didn't give me much. I'm guessing that's because he doesn't give a shit. I'm hoping that you do."

"Maybe. But don't get your hopes up, and don't be too hard on Lt. Welton. Like all of us, he's seen thousands of murders. Exactly 3,167 since I came onboard. After awhile they just become numbers on a board. It's the only way you can survive and stay sane," he said, his face grave.

"Fair enough. I'm still interested in hearing what you've got to say, though."

"That's going to take some time," he said with a tired sigh. He pointed towards the intersection of Eleventh and H Streets. "Every night that corner is a major open-air drug market. A group of older addicts sell crack and heroin there. Eric knew most of them."

"Really. How do you know that?" I asked, interrupting his flow. He looked mildly annoyed.

"Shit...I knew Eric since grade school. Everyone around here did. And everyone knows the corner dealers, too. You can't live in a place your whole life and not get known. Anyway, the corner dealers said that Eric used to walk home from work every day. He would go over the H Street Bridge and turn left right there at the intersection. He lived just north of here. He was only three blocks from home when they got him."

"It must have been rough, pulling up on the scene and seeing Eric like that."

"Yeah, it was. Just when you think you seen so much that you can't be shocked no more, somethin' happens that rips your guts out. When I pulled up, it was about seven in the evening. A small group of people were standing around the body. They stepped aside as I came forward, and there he was, laying on the grass right there across the street. It was more than just seeing him ripped up; I'm pretty used to that. It was the fact that he never did anything to anyone. He was one of the good people, truly. If a guy's been killed, and he was slinging dope and rippin' people off, it's hard not to feel like he got what he deserved. But Eric....he was always helpin' people out. His main hobby was goin' to church. That's what made me mad."

"Is there any word on the street about who might have done it?"

"No. That's the spooky part. There was nothing. On many of the killings we investigate, shit, half the neighborhood knows who did it 30 minutes after it happens. You put yourself out there and talk to the right people and you going to know too, real quick. May not be able to prove it or get any witnesses to testify, but you almost always know who did it."

"Really," I said. "How does the word get around so fast?"

"Well, a lot of times tensions have been building between the victim and his killer for quite awhile, and there's plenty of time and trash talk that let's people know what's comin'. Also, you got a lot of these dope fiends spendin' ten and twelve hours a day on the corners. A lot of gossip gets done between drug buys. Also, we got snitches on almost every other block. We look out for them and don't bust them on petty shit, and they provide us with information, off the record. Point us in the right direction when we don't know where to start. They rarely testify though; that would be death."

"Doesn't it burn you up that the person who killed Eric was never caught?"

He looked at me for a second before answering. "Well, you get used to that too. Four in ten of our homicides go unsolved. It's actually harder when you know who did it, and can't prove it, and have to see the bastard on the corner every day laughing at you. Of course, there is some street justice that can be arranged in those situations, but I don't have no part of that."

"Lt. Welton told me that someone saw the car used in the drive-by."

"Yeah, one of the dope fiends on the corner saw it. He said it was a gold Lexus and that it was parked on the curb right there." Connel pointed right across the street from us, where Eric was shot.

"Shit!" I exclaimed. "They were waiting for him! They must have known the route he walked home every night. They rolled down the window as he walked past and started firing. No wonder it did so much damage. They opened up at point-blank range."

"Yeah. Then they did a U-turn and took off north, away from H street," Connel added.

"And you guys think it was a case of mistaken identity? That close? When they were sitting there waiting for him on the route he walked home every night?"

"Sure, it's possible. Especially if they were local hitters hired by someone, going on a sketchy description."

"But he was wearing a suit and tie. He was carrying a briefcase."

"Oh please. That don't necessarily mean nothing. Most of the dealers in the city are small-time, working stiffs trying to make a little extra cash. If they were after someone like that, maybe someone who owed some money, they might have thought that Eric was him. Hey, I know it's a stretch, but it's the only explanation at this point. Like I said...I know these streets and everyone in them. I talked to everyone. No one had it in for Eric. No one had *any reason* to have it in for Eric."

I spent the rest of the day interviewing two other members of the family, Eric's maternal uncle and sister. They confirmed that Eric had been reliable and decent. They agreed that no one could possibly have wanted to kill him. I also learned that Eric had run a good 800 in college, had become disillusioned with the Redskins (they were on a losing streak then), loved Star Trek (the original), and was saving money to buy a home. Unfortunately, no one mentioned anything that sounded even vaguely like a clue.

-4-

Avignon Fre'res is a couple of blocks down from my old Columbia Road apartment. I was looking at the menu and trying to distract myself from the fact that I had $52.38 in the bank.

"Do you want me to pay?" asked Aislinn.

She was a Stanford graduate, who worked for the Commerce Department. Long red hair, alabaster skin, gorgeous almond shaped eyes and perfect features. Her parents had immigrated from Ireland when she was ten, but you would hardly know it. She had embraced America absolutely. The only traces of her heritage were her beautiful Celtic name and charming Dublin accent that was faint almost to the point of being imperceptible. I had called her earlier from a pay phone to let her know I was in town and see if she wanted to have dinner. She did.

"How about dutch?" she asked.

"Ok."

"I don't mind paying," she said, trying again.

"Dutch is fine."

"I hope you're not refusing out of some misguided sense of machismo."

"It's not that," I replied. "It's more of an issue of independence. I don't like to burden other people with the consequences of my choices. A person loses something when they do that."

She thought about that for a second and then smiled. "Well, at least you know I'm not with you for your money."

"That raises the question. Why are you with me?" I said facetiously.

I looked at her face, surprised to see that she was seriously pondering the question.

"Aislinn, I was joking. I didn't really expect an answer," I told her.

"I want to answer. It gives me a chance to tell you some things I was thinking about while I was away."

She paused and then said, "At first you were a mystery to me, and to some extent, you still are. I've never met a man like you, and that intrigues me. For instance, you're not afraid to live exactly the way you want to. Most people aren't like that. They stay in jobs they hate because they're afraid to lose their health insurance. They never paint that picture or write that song because they're afraid of what other people will think. They live every day enslaved to a hundred petty anxieties that sap their energy and kill their dreams. I like being with you because somehow you've managed to be free without sacrificing decency."

She paused, then her face broke into a beautiful smile. "Plus, you got a good referral," she said, half-joking.

"I think I know who by."

She nodded. We had met through Susan, her former roommate. Susan's parents had hired me to scare away an ex-boyfriend, who was stalking her. I took care of the old boyfriend, but Susan was so freaked by the incident that she moved back home.

"So how is she doing?" I asked.

"She's still in Minneapolis, living with her parents. She's eternally grateful to you, but never wants to step foot in this city again."

"That's the second time I've heard that today," I said. "Let her know I checked up on that guy a couple of months ago. He's still living in Georgetown."

"She'll be glad to know. I'm sure she still has nightmare's about him showing up one day in Minneapolis."

The waiter came and took our order. Aislinn looked out the plate glass window. I surreptitiously enjoyed her profile, the line of her neck.

"I missed you while you were away," I told her. She had been gone for two months on a temporary assignment in the Middle East. "How did you like it over there?"

"It made me glad I live here." She looked into my eyes and twined her fingers in mine. "I missed you too."

We talked some more about her trip until the waiter brought my eggs benedict and black coffee and her pasta dish and wine. The waiter offered me cream and sugar.

I refused. Black coffee is perfect and should not be tampered with.

The waiter nodded, asked if we needed anything else, and then left. I started in on my food, thinking that one of the two things I liked about this place was the fact that they served breakfast all day. The other was that the interior looked like an ancient Parisian café.

"By the way," Aislinn said, "I just found out I'll be going to Hong Kong with the Undersecretary in July. Maybe you could solve a couple of cases real quick and come with me."

"I'd love to, but I've only got one case, no leads, and very few good ideas about how to proceed next."

"That's a promising start."

"Isn't it."

We spent the rest of the evening riding around the city on my motorcycle, stopping as the spirit moved us. We laid on our backs in the grass and watched with slowly rising elation as it rained cherry blossoms, a gorgeous, softly swirling cloud of pink and white that came to rest in pleasing disarray on the majestic, emerald sweep of the Mall. The warm wind whispered like a quiet-voiced revelation, intermittently rising to a crescendo that lifted the petals off the cherry trees and filled the spring air with the smell of azaleas.

We sat on the steps of the Lincoln Memorial, looking out as the fading sunlight sparkled in a shimmering wake on the reflecting pool and sun-fired the soaring, immaculate column of the Washington Monument to a brilliant white.

We caught a midnight show at the Uptown, sitting in my favorite seats in the balcony and drank coffee on the bank of the Potomac at four a.m., soothed by the sound of it's softly rolling waters.

At eight a.m. I dropped her off at the building where she worked, on Constitution Avenue.

I woke in the early afternoon in Aislinn's apartment. I made the bed, then went out onto the fire escape, and smoked a cigarette while looking out over the city. Aislinn's apartment was on the top floor of a building just off Eighteenth Street Northwest, so I could see a long way out over an immense sea of rooftops. You could just see the tip of the Washington Monument peeking up over the horizon. Clouds drifted

27

J.D. Miller

lazily in an azure sky. Below was the bustle on the Adams Morgan restaurant strip.

I'd read somewhere that detectives solved cases by thinking about them. I thought about the case awhile. Nothing occurred to me.

I looked out over the city some more and thought about how it was really three cities. The first was the Washington of the monuments and the Mall, the White House and Smithsonians. Majestic, uncommonly beautiful and embodying a serene grandeur. Designed to intimidate and impress foreign heads of state, seen nightly in millions of homes as the backdrop for the evening news. Sullied only by the discordant rhythm of the tourists. Georgetown could be thought of as its suburb.

The second was here in Northwest D.C. Bustling, ethnically diverse, often bohemian. A feast of hundreds of eccentric restaurants, galleries, bookstores, avant-garde movie houses, and coffee shops. Dupont Circle, Woodley Park, Cleveland Park and Adams Morgan. Home to the young and hip, artists, graduate students, gay men, perpetually single women, immigrants, low-level government employees, anti-government radicals, and all sorts of other free spirits living in a cultural patchwork of their own design. Former home to one private investigator, who got sick of the noise and neurosis and moved to the country. It was fun to visit though. You can't get Ethiopian food in the Shenandoah, or see Lyle Mays play at Blues Alley.

The third city was comprised of Northeast and Southeast D.C. It was where Eric Jones had lived, and was referred to in the media as the "murder capital of the world."

I heard the door in the apartment open, and a moment later Aislinn's head peeked out the window. Her eyes were bloodshot, and she looked exhausted.

"Hi. I came home early to get some sleep," she said blearily. "I adore you, but if you wake me I will shoot you with your own gun."

"I'll keep that in mind if I ever want to commit suicide."

She leaned out further, gave me a kiss, then into her bedroom and closed the door.

-5-

The US Government Printing Office is in a six-story, square, ocher-colored building a few blocks down from the Capitol. I walked in through double doors set beneath a soaring archway, signed in at the security desk, and took an elevator to the basement.

I got off the elevator with a couple of people who were gossiping about a co-worker, and entered a room that ran the length of the building. It was lit by high-powered fluorescent lights that flooded the work area with a sickly glow, washing out colors and eliminating the possibility of shadows. It was crammed from end-to-end with various large machines, each of which hummed like some giant species of insect. The cumulative sound was deafening. My keen detective's mind told me they were probably used in some way for printing. Numerous workers were hovering over the machines with a dull, mindless absorption, engaged in an assortment of unrecognizable tasks.

There was an office at the far-side of the basement, and I made my way towards it, threading a path through the machines. I stopped at a desk in front of the office, behind which a young woman sat typing away rapidly at a computer.

"Can I help you?" she asked. She had a faint accent that was hard to recognize over the din of the machines, long flowing jet black hair, and big beautiful eyes that were partially concealed by reading glasses.

"My name is Mark Christian. I'm a private investigator." I handed her my license. "Could I speak to your supervisor please?"

She took the license and looked at it, her eyes widening behind the glasses. As she handed it back to me, she said, "May I give him the reason?" I had it now; the accent was South American.

"I want to talk to him about Eric Jones."

"Just a moment." She got up and went through the office door, closing it behind her. She came out a minute later, and I watched her as she did, deciding that her body was as good as her face.

"He's making a call and will be with you in a minute," she informed me.

To pass the time, we made some polite conversation.

"Where are you from?" I asked.

"Ecuador."

"How long have you been in the States?"

"Three years."

I still remembered some Spanish from the seminary so I asked, gesturing vaguely towards the machines, "*Como aguanta usted el ruido?*"

She smiled and said, "After a couple of months, you don't really hear it anymore."

She started to say something else when her boss walked out of the office. He was white, medium height, undistinguished looking, but had the air of a man who was the master of his little universe. A big fish in a small pond.

We shook hands, and he said, "Phil Riley. Why don't we talk in my office?"

The office, like the man, was ordinary, filled with an assortment of bland government-issue office furniture. The only personal touch was a poster of Maui tacked to the wall behind the desk.

31

"So, are you investigating Eric's death?" he asked as we sat down.

"Yes."

"Who hired you?" he asked.

"His mother."

"Oh, sure. I met her at the funeral. What a waste it was, what happened to him. No one around here could believe it when we first heard."

"Well, I appreciate you taking the time to see me."

"Anything I can do to help," he said sincerely.

"How about giving me your impressions of Eric."

He paused, gathering his thoughts and then said, "I was his direct supervisor for eight years. Eric was the best floor manager I ever had. He was conscientious and always had a positive attitude. Most of the people who worked for him liked him from what I could tell."

Once again I was getting nowhere. The unwritten social contract against speaking ill of the dead was good and right for family and friends, but bad for investigators with no leads.

"That's pretty much what everyone has been telling me, that he was a great guy. I don't doubt that. But it doesn't help me. If I'm going to find out who did this, it may be helpful to find out about the whole person. We all have faults. What were Eric's, in your opinion?"

"Well," he said, wanting to cooperate but clearly uncomfortable, "the only fault I can think of was that sometimes he was too much a stickler for procedure. Refused to be flexible sometimes. You have to have high standards for your employees, but you also have to allow them to be human. Especially in this work. As you can imagine, it's not the most exciting job in the world." He paused, his face darkening with concern.

32

"Is this confidential? Are you going to be interviewing my boss?"

"That would be 'yes' and 'no.'"

"Good," he said, relaxing a bit.

"Could you give me an example of what you're talking about?"

"Take smoke breaks," he said. "I realized years ago that for a lot of my employees, it's the only thing they look forward to all day. So if they spend an extra five minutes out there smoking, I don't make a big deal out of it. That's, of course, assuming that the work is getting done. But for Eric, if the smoke breaks were supposed to be ten minutes, you better not be coming in eleven minutes later. We disagreed about his approach on many occasions, behind closed doors of course, but for Eric right and wrong were absolutes. If you had ten minutes, you took ten minutes. Period."

I was liking this guy more by the minute. Apparently, there was a human being underneath the bureaucratic exterior. His bland office and manner were probably a sort of self-protective camouflage he used to blend in and keep attention off himself.

"Any unstable employees who might 'go postal' over Eric's inflexibility?"

"No," he said. "We've got plenty of unstable employees, but I couldn't imagine any of them killing someone. But then again, you never know nowadays, do you?"

"I guess not. Anything else, any rumors, jealousy, or conflicts on the job?"

"No," he said, gazing into the distance as he pondered the question. "But I'm not exactly the guy that people would come to with rumors. Frankly, I'm a little surprised at your line of questioning. I talked to Eric's mother a few months after he was murdered, and she said the police thought that some druggies had done it. Mistook him for someone else in the dark. Why are you looking here?"

"Just covering all the bases. The police probably got it right, but I want to make sure I look into all of the possibilities. So, what kind of stuff do you print here?"

"Yearly reports, budgets, all congressional records, passports, you name it," he said.

"You're right. Sounds pretty boring."

"It's a living."

On the trip home I went from plains to hills to mountains and from buildings to houses to farms. It took two hours.

That evening I sat on my porch, gazing out over the green valley framed by mountains. It was almost dark. What remained of the sun was a diadem of orange light that softly lit the treetops and crowned the hills to the west. I stayed out there till all the stars were out, Rachel curled up contentedly beside me, then got up and went inside to read in bed.

Just as I settled in, the phone rang. It was Lillian Jones.

"Mr. Christian," she said in her gravelly voice. "Have you found anythin' out?"

"Not yet, but I'll keep at it."

"Well I'm glad you're in. My son—the one I was telling you about that's an officer in the Army—is visiting this weekend. Since you said you wanted to interview the whole family, I thought you might want to talk to him."

"Sounds good. Tell him to meet me in front of the 4 & 20 Blackbird restaurant in Flint Hill tomorrow morning at ten."

"He'll be there."

The next morning I got on my Triumph and started towards Flint Hill. A low grey-and-white ceiling of clouds had moved in overnight, muting the light and gently caressing the mountaintops, sifting through the emerald trees to emerge in eddies and swirls of white mist. It settled in the hollows and softly receded when approached. I drove through a tunnel of leaves, formed by the overarching boughs of dogwoods that hugged the road and passed a field of tiger lilies, swaying gently in the warm breeze. The road was like a gray river winding through a canyon of leaves until it opened up on Main Street in Flint Hill.

William Jones was waiting when I arrived. He stood up smartly as I walked onto the restaurant's porch and shook my hand. He was a large man, about six-two, and was clearly in good shape. He had close-cropped hair, a face that was all hard angles, and exuded an air of intelligence and unforced strength and authority.

"Hi, I'm Will. Eric's brother."

"Mark Christian, nice to meet you. Ever been here before?"

"No. This is my first time visiting my mom since she moved to the country."

"Well, you're in for a treat."

We went inside, got seated, and made small talk. Within a half hour we were eating breakfast. I was having the salmon eggs benedict and Kenyan coffee.

"So you're in the Army?" I asked. "West Point or OCS?"

"What makes you think I'm an officer?" he replied lightly.

"I was an E-5 in the Marines. After a while you learn to recognize an officer in or out of uniform."

He chuckled. "Keeps you out of trouble, right?"

"Yeah, and keeps you out of shit work."

"That's true. To answer your question, I came in through the Point. How about you?"

"Quantico for basic, Bravo 11, eventually landed in Recon."

"Tough duty," he said. "Spend any time overseas?"

"Iraq and Mogadishu."

He nodded. "I did some time in Iraq. Commanded the 1/7 mechanized battalion, 24th Infantry Division under General McCaffery."

"Didn't you guys see some major action at the Euphrates?" I asked.

"Yes, but it was pretty much a turkey shoot. The Abrams has almost twice the range of the tanks the Iraqis were using, so we could stand off at a safe distance and take them out one by one. They never had a chance...and that's the way I like it."

"I agree. A true victory is bringing most of your guys home in one piece. Let the other guy die for his country."

"Amen," he said. I lost two guys at the Euphrates, both of whom were killed in accidents. I'd have preferred zero, but that's pretty unprecedented for a major battle between opposing armies. How about you? What were you doing during the 'late unpleasantness.'"

"I was running around the desert with my Recon unit, looking for Scuds. Didn't find any."

"Hmmm. How about Mogadishu? I thought that was an Army show."

"It was. I was on TDY to the Rangers. One of those inter-service exchange programs. I was with Chalk 4 during the battle."

He nodded. "I was in Korea, pissed off I was missing the show. Changed my mind, though, after I heard about how bad it was."

"It was bad. The whole city was shooting at us. It was the longest sustained firefight since the Vietnam war." I pulled up my sleeve slightly to show him a long horizontal scar on my upper bicep. "I got this trying to get to the guys in Blackhawk Super Six Four after it was shot down. Two other slugs hit my vest, broke a rib, and knocked me silly for a minute. This little Spec 4 ran into the street and dragged me to safety. I decided then and there that maybe you Army guys were all right after all."

Will smiled. "We have our moments."

We swapped war stories for a few more minutes and then got down to business.

"So, you want to ask me about my brother."

"Yes" I said. "What was he like?"

"Well, to know my brother you've got to know my mother. How old do you think she is?"

"Late sixties," I guessed.

"She's 54. Looks older 'cause she wore herself out working two and three jobs to support us. Came home and still took time to check our homework. Took us to church every Sunday. Didn't allow us to play in the streets like the other kids. Eric had her determination and work ethic. He was also devout like her. He became a deacon in his church. He was also like mom in that once he set his mind to something, just get out of the way, 'cause that was how it was going to be."

"I was surprised to hear that he never moved out of Southeast. He must have made enough money to do so."

"He did," Will said, sighing. "We urged him to move on many occasions, but he wouldn't even consider it. Like I said, once he made up his mind about something..."

"But you did."

"Yes, and at the time it was one of the hardest things I've ever done. The day I shipped off to West Point was the first day I had ever left the city. Prior to that, I had never even been across the river to Virginia! It was like walking off the edge of the world. People don't realize, when you spend your whole life in ten square blocks of a city, it gets real easy to stay, no matter how bad it is. You know that old saying about how people will choose the hell they know over the heaven they don't know. It's definitely true. You develop an unconscious fear of the outside world or assume that it's the same everywhere because that's all you know or can imagine. And of course, there's the attachment to your friends and family…"

"So are you saying that's why Eric stayed?" I asked.

"No. That's how it is with most people, me included, but with Eric it was probably a mix of idealism and incredible stubbornness."

"I never had the opportunity to get attached to a place like that," I said, surprised at how comfortable I felt opening up to this man. It was an uncommon feeling for me. "My parents died when I was young so I went to live with an aunt and uncle. He turned out to be an alcoholic, who beat on me. My aunt pretended that nothing was happening. He threw me out the first time I got old enough to beat on him back. Then I went into the Catholic seminary."

"You're kidding. You studied to be a priest?!" he asked in amazement.

"I kid you not. Stayed four years in a seminary in northwest Pennsylvania."

"With that background, I'm surprised the Marines didn't send you into the chaplains corps."

I laughed. "I never thought of that. They never tried, thank God. I would have made the world's worst chaplain."

"So why'd you leave the seminary?"

"Celibacy was just not working for me."

"When you got out, did you make up for lost time?" he asked, smiling wickedly.

"And then some," I said emphatically.

"Well," he said, serious again. "I'm glad you gave that drunk uncle of yours what he had coming."

"Put him in the hospital for a week."

I pulled a piece of paper out of my pocket and handed it to Will. As he read it, I said, "These are the people I'm going to interview. Is there anyone else you can think of who I should talk to?"

He gazed at the paper for a minute, then handed it back and said, "You might want to talk to my cousin Carla. Last time I heard she was still living with her boyfriend in Southeast near the Navy Yard. She's not on the list because no one has talked to her in years.

She been runnin' the streets since she was fourteen. Been in and out of drug treatment a dozen times. She was cut off when she began to steal from family members to support her habit. If anyone has heard some word on the street about who killed Eric, it's her. But I've got to warn you; it's a long-shot that she heard anything, and it's going to be dangerous."

"I've got no leads, so I guess I better give it a shot," I said.

"Want some help? I got another week around here before I have to report back to duty."

"Thanks, but no way. That's my job. Besides, you're mother's only got one son left. I'd feel pretty guilty if something happened to you."

-6-

Later that day I sat on my front porch, gazing absently at the vista of mountains and meadows, colored in brushstrokes of green. Talking about my past with Will this morning had caused some long-suppressed memories to swim up from the basement of consciousness. For futile minutes, without success, I fought the flood of memory. Soon I was drowning in them. I was remembering the day that I lost the fear of death.

I was a part of the international peace-keeping force in Mogadishu, Somalia. We were there to secure the delivery of food to the starving people in the countryside, but soon after arriving, we learned that it was being hoarded by an assortment of petty warlords.

On October 3rd, 1993, we roped down from helicopters into a market area in the heart of Mogadishu. Our mission was to capture two of the top people blocking the delivery of food and bring them back to base. Within minutes, we were being fired at from every direction, with people running from all parts of the city to join the fight. We were pinned down all night. By the time we were extracted the next morning, eighteen Americans were dead and seventy wounded.

The memories were surreal and scattered, like the afterimages from a hallucinogenic-induced dream. Crawling on the wasted streets of Mogadishu, face down so low it scrapped on the gravel, a hurricane of bullets, RPG's, horror roaring all around in a supersonic, out-of-control, never-ending scream.

41

Snapshot images of hell, blood spurting from wounds, the red spaghetti twist of spilled entrails, scattered limbs. Sanity strained like a gossamer sheet stretched to breaking until I crawled up on a friend lying with his chest gaping open spitting up blood and he stared a thousand miles up into heaven and said "I'm ready," and then let go and smiled as the breath left him. Up and running to move forward and then lying down. *How did I get on my back?* Feeling my heart stop from shock and then rising up. Looking down on my body, eyes rolled back in my head, vest smoking from the rounds that had stitched me.

Quiet now and total peace. Death, the ultimate medevac, the ultimate dope. *"Good to know it all ends ok,"* I thought. Seeing my friend move from his annihilated body, a sun-diamond spirit whole again, into a circle of beautiful white light. At that moment I realized that the worst thing that can happen is that you will die, and that's not bad at all. We do indeed rest in peace, because there is a beauty beyond the ugliness of the world. It's holding on to life too tightly that causes most fear.

Then into my body again, as if snapped awake, a hand gripping my sleeve with frightening intensity as it dragged me into the cover of an alley.

"MEDIC! JESUS FUCKIN' CHRIST MEDIC!" a voice screamed hysterically.

I reached up and grabbed my savior's collar gently and said calmly, smiling, "It's ok. It's really all ok. Afterwards I mean. Everything is going to be fine."

He turns to a guy next to him, with a puzzled look on his face, and says, "Fucker must have been hit in the head; he's gone crazy."

I start laughing hysterically; it's the funniest thing I've ever heard, rolling from side-to-side and kicking my feet until a sharp pain in my chest brings me down to a chuckle.

A medic looms over me suddenly, face stiff with urgent concern, his hands splattered with blood and dirt, screaming over the sound of incoming rounds, "Where are you hit?!"

I didn't respond, enraptured as I was with new-found revelation.

The medic ripped my vest off and ran his hands over my body, rolling me onto my side to check for exit wounds. "You're going to be all right," he yelled over the roar of nearby gunfire. "The vest stopped two slugs and the third just grazed your arm! Do you have any pain in your chest!?"

"Yeah. A sharp pain on my left side," I said, completely back now from the next world.

"You probably got a couple of broken ribs when the slugs hit. Don't move; you might puncture someth...."

There was an explosion of red rain and the medic flew back, his head blown apart. A Somali stood in the mouth of the alley, firing an AK-47 on full auto, spraying us with bullets. Two more Rangers went down before I could raise my M-16 and put him down with a three round burst into his chest.

Before that day, they used to call me "jarhead," the traditional derogatory nickname that the Rangers used for Marines. But after we got back and the story of what I'd said after being hit spread around the battalion, they started calling me "Buddha."

When I got home from Somalia, I caught a plane to Washington, D.C. and sought out my best friend Greg, knowing that he was the only person who could help me deal with what had happened. We had met in our early teens in the Seminary and rapidly become inseparable, but unlike me, he stayed the course and eventually became a priest. I knew intuitively when I first saw him that he was the best human being I would ever meet. At a time when I had lost my faith in humanity, his decency had restored it.

I found him at his parish downtown on T street. After a long hug, he took me to his private quarters in the back. The walls of his room were ancient stone, adorned with only a large crucifix and the prism of light projected from the stained glass window. I sat down in a musty old chair and lit up a cigarette. Smoke soon drifted in a swirling cloud of grey and white about the ceiling.

"You've taken up smoking," he said without judgment.

"Yes."

I told him everything that had happened, and he listened without interruption for over an hour, his eyes emanating compassion and concern. Silent tears ran down his face as I described being shot and dying and coming back.

Finally I finished, and there was a long silence.

He said "I prayed every day you were over there. How has this affected you? Are you all right?"

"I'm at peace now with the idea of my own death, but I killed many people. It makes me feel dirty in a way that I'm afraid will never go away."

"Perhaps that's not a bad thing," he said softly.

"What do you mean?" I asked, feeling a brief flash of anger.

He paused to put his thoughts together and then said, "You can move towards evil in many ways: by refusing to let go of feelings like hatred and envy, or by refusing to hold onto feelings like remorse. You become evil if you let yourself become indifferent to the sufferings of others, even those who are trying to hurt you. However painful it may feel to harbor that remorse, to bear the burdens of conscience, it is the one thing that will keep you from becoming less than what you are. I believe that you had to do what you did, and that it was for a good cause, but that remorse for killing is a good thing."

There was another long pause while I digested his words.

Then I said, "I saw some horrible things. Sometimes the Somalis held children in front of them as a shield while they fired at us. I guess they thought that we wouldn't fire back if they were holding the children. I still have trouble imagining a mind that could do something like that."

"To care about others is to hurt sometimes," he said. "In hard places in the world some people let go of caring about anyone or anything because it hurts too much. In places where people die every day of starvation and disease and violence, life becomes cheap. They think that to allow themselves to care will cause a level of hurt that will be unbearable and drive them insane. Some even let go of caring about children. It is disgusting, but it is very human and has been happening since the beginning of time."

He paused to think and then continued. "Your profession is much more difficult than mine, spiritually speaking. You make your living applying violence, which is terrible and repugnant to me, but sometimes necessary. Our use of violence stopped the Holocaust and brought peace to Bosnia. As insane as it was, the threat of mutual destruction probably averted a third world war with the Russians. As long as you only use violence to protect others—those who can't protect themselves, and never come to glorify it or enjoy it after the fact—you will be able to maintain your decency."

"But what if my next mission is one that I don't believe in?" I said. "One that's not about protecting people or doing some humanitarian deed? As a Marine, I won't have a choice but to kill anyway. Plus I'm not always in a position to have enough facts to make a decision about whether the mission is right or not. A call comes in the middle of the night and you go. Now that I've seen the things I've seen, I'm not sure I could live with myself if I was not absolutely sure that it was for a good cause."

I paused and he remained silent, listening. We had known each other so long that he already knew what I was working up to.

"And you know me, I've never been good with authority. I'm thinking about getting out of the Marines. I want something where I have more autonomy, something where I can pick and choose the missions."

"Like what?" he asked.

"I don't know yet. I'll let you know when I figure it out."

The visions receded into a corner of my mind, and I became conscious again of sitting in the rocker on my front porch, the smell of grass and flowers, the warm wind caressing my face. I picked up my tea to take a sip and stopped halfway, looking at my hand in surprise. It was shaking.

-7-

A New Life Clinic was in a non-descript, tan building about six blocks from the Capitol. I rode the elevator to the top floor, entered a modern waiting area, and checked in with the receptionist. Almost immediately I was shown into the office of James DeMello, substance abuse counselor.

He came around the side of his desk, and we shook hands. He grinned and said, "What the hell are you doing here?"

"Is that a line you use with all your patients?"

"Damn," he said with mock concern, "that's why they're not getting better." Actually, a mutual friend had told me that James was one of the best drug counselors in the city.

"Let me guess," he continued. "You've finally decided to quit smoking, and you've come to me for help."

In response, I took a pack of Salems out of my jacket, tapped one out with a flick of my wrist, and put it in my mouth.

"Then again, maybe you're here for another reason," he said wryly.

"Gosh, you shrinks sure are good at reading body language," I said as I replaced the cigarettes and took a look around. We had been friends for a long time, but I had never seen his office. It was tastefully done in dark wood and burgundy. There were framed prints and degrees on the walls, a floor-to-ceiling window, and hanging plants. On his desk was a framed picture of his wife, an attractive blond holding a baby, who seemed to have inherited the best parts of both parents.

"I need some help on a case. Where would you look for an addict that no one has seen for the last two years?"

"The morgue." James said, his face serious now.

"That's it?" I asked.

"That would be my best guess. My second would be jail. Least likely is that he or she is somewhere on the streets."

"Well, I can check into the morgue and the jail with a couple of calls. Want to get together for a drink tonight?"

"Sure. I'm out of here at 7:30. The usual?"

"Sounds good."

That evening I was sitting at the bar of the Café Latrec, smoking a cigarette and staring idly at the rainbow pyramid of liquor bottles that lay against the far wall. They were backlit with a deep emerald-green light that gave the bar area a strangely surreal glow. The café itself was dimly lit and smoky with dark wood tables and walls. A loose, rolling four-piece jazz ensemble played on the stereo, with soft edges and a groove that rose and fell like waves on the ocean. And over it all, the din of conversation floated like a fifth instrument.

"Donald Bird, isn't it?" I said to the bartender as she poured me a finger of Jack Daniels. The amber liquid splashed into the glass with a pleasing sound.

"Yeah. You know your jazz. Are you a musician?"

"No. Just a fan."

"Oh." She said, looking slightly disappointed. "Waiting for someone?"

"Yep. How could you tell?"

"People who aren't usually have a faintly desperate look."

I smiled. She was tall, ugly and very attractive all at the same time. I was pondering this strange phenomenon when James walked in with his easy, purposeful stride. He glanced around as he came towards me, taking in the place.

I got up to greet him and he said, "Let's take a seat at a table. I hate the bar."

"Sure."

We took a table towards the back.

I said, "How's the baby?"

"Fine. Growing every day."

"And Diane?"

"Tired mostly."

"That's understandable."

He nodded in agreement. "You have no idea."

"Nor do I want to," I said quickly and firmly.

"Does Aislinn know that?"

"She starting to get the idea."

"And you're afraid that she won't like it," he said with complete certainty.

"Yes." I was surprised. I was not used to being read that easily. But that's what you get when a shrink is one of your good friends. "I have a feeling that the longer we know each other, the less my lifestyle will appeal to her."

"Well, I can't say I'm surprised. Most women like to flirt with your side of life, but they rarely want to marry it."

I paused before responding, leaning forward to light another cigarette with the candle that flickered dimly on the table.

"So you think we're doomed to fail."

"It's a definite possibility."

"You know," I said lightly, "most of the time I like the fact that you're a straight-shooter, but sometimes it can be a pain in the ass."

"Ignorance is bliss?" he said, smiling now.

"It can be. Maybe we wouldn't have moments of bliss without it."

"I agree in some sense. I doubt it's true in relationships."

"Keep thine eyes wide open before marriage and half-closed afterwards?" I asked, quoting the old adage.

"Exactly."

It took me a moment to respond because I was distracted by a girl at the next table. She was stunning, with perfect features and long raven hair that swept down her back in a loose curve. She was smoking a Marlboro with swift, sure movements and pretending to be interested in a friend's conversation. We exchanged a long glance, and then she looked away.

I said, "Maybe it wouldn't be so bad."

"What?"

"If Aislinn and I didn't work out." I felt guilty saying it. "I do love the feeling that anything can happen."

James smiled broadly. "I know. If you got married, I wouldn't have anyone to live vicariously through."

"By the way," I said, changing the subject, "After I left your office, I called the morgue and the cops, and they have no record of the person I'm looking for. There were a couple of unidentified Jane Does at the morgue, but both were over fifty, which is too old to be the woman I'm looking for. The cops said that she has had a long string of arrests, but confirmed that she isn't currently locked up. So that eliminates two of your guesses. Any idea on how I can go about checking out the third?"

"You mean the possibility that she may still be runnin' the streets?"

"Yes."

"Can you tell me more about who you're looking for? That may help with a recommendation."

"She's the cousin of a guy named Eric Jones, who was killed in a drive-by. The family has asked me to investigate his murder. The cousin's name is Carla. Nobody has seen her for a couple of years. Apparently, the family cut her off after she started stealing from them. She's been on drugs since the age of fourteen, starting with crack and graduating later to heroin."

"Do you think she murdered her cousin? Is that why you want to find her?"

I shook my head and said, "I just want to ask her some questions. I've been told that she knows the streets inside and out and might have heard something about who killed Eric. It's a long-shot, but I've got nothing else at this point."

"Well," James said, staring into the distance as he thought the problem through, "strolling down to Southeast and asking questions on the corners is not going to get you anywhere. The minute they see a young white guy like you, they'll think you're 5.0, and no one will talk to you."

"'5.0?"

"Yeah, 5.0. As in *Hawaii 5.0.* It's street slang for cop."

"Oh."

"You need someone to vouch for you, someone known and trusted on the street, someone with impeccable street credentials," he said. "And I've got just the guy."

-8-

Mother's restaurant is a D.C. icon, saturated in the smells and sounds of its incomparable, eternally frying breakfast. I had arranged to meet Sterling Jacobs here, a recovering heroin addict, whom James had recommended as the perfect street chaperone.

I'd been there twenty minutes and was just finishing my third cup of coffee when Sterling walked in. He looked to be in his late fifties, with graying hair and a tired body, but a relatively unlined face.

He spotted me easily (being the only white guy in a ten-block radius) and came over and introduced himself, taking a seat across from me. Before we could get any further, the owner of the place, "Mother," recognized Sterling and came flying away from the grill to pull him into a bear-hug.

There were more greetings and affectionate banter before she said, "What can Mother get you boys?"

I ordered an omelet with a side of scrapple, and Sterling asked for the double stack of pancakes and a decaf coffee.

"So you're the private eye," he said, looking me over after Mother left.

"Yep."

"Mr. DeMello spoke highly of you."

"Really. I'm surprised. He usually busts my balls."

Sterling laughed. "Well, he did say that you was addicted to danger the way that I'm addicted to drugs."

"And the worst part is that he's usually right," I observed.

"Don't I know it. He was my counselor for two years. I been on the receiving end more times than you can count. Just what I needed—to tell you the truth."

"Really? I thought counselors were supposed to be all soft and cuddly."

"Not drug counselors," he said. "The good ones get in your face and tell you all the things you don't want to hear. Helps break through the denial. But they can do it without being mean or petty. With the good ones, you can tell that they doin' it for you, cause they care about you."

"Sounds like you've had quite a few counselors," I said.

"Oh yes. I've been in and out of treatment most of my adult life. Didn't take till this last time. Been clean goin' on four years now."

"Congratulations."

"Thanks, but I still got a long way to go," he said sternly, as if reminding himself.

"How many addicts relapse?" I asked, following his line of thought.

"I'd say about nine out of ten. Of all the people I was in treatment with, only me and one other guy are still clean that I know of for sure."

"Damn! Are you serious?" I asked. "I had no idea it was that bad."

"Oh yeah. This is a tough disease to beat 'cause it turns your mind against you. Once you catch a habit, it becomes like a basic need; you want and need it like you need food or air. And of course livin' around here don't help. There's so much of it right out in the open. I get offered drugs just walkin' down the street. It's like trying to go on a diet while livin' in the grocery store."

Suddenly a waitress leaned over us, put our plates down, and made a graceful exit.

I stared down at the fluffiest, fattest, most perfect omelet I'd ever seen and scrapple that was cooked just right (a shade past medium). Every cholesterol-craving part of my brain sang for joy. "I think I just fell in love with Mother," I said to Sterling.

He chuckled politely while dumping syrup on his pancakes.

"So how are you different? How are you able to stay clean when everyone else went back onto drugs?" I asked as we began to eat.

"Well, for one thing I learned how to live the serenity prayer. *Really live it.* Lots of people can mouth it, but I live it. Do you know it?"

"Sure. God grant me the serenity to accept the things I cannot change, the courage to change the things I can..."

"*And the wisdom to know the difference,*" he said, finishing it for me. "That last part is the most important part. Learning what we can and cannot change. You can do a lifetime of growth just on that one idea."

He paused to pull his thoughts together, then said "Most addicts can never let go of the hope that somehow, someday they can change the facts of addiction. That someday they can learn how to control their drug use, 'cause if they can control it, then they can avoid the consequences. Usually they think they can control it through willpower. Never works for long. When people relapse, they aren't thinkin', 'Oh I'll go back to bein' a junkie now.' No, they're thinkin', 'Just this one hit won't hurt.' Of course, 'just this one' always leads to another and another. Or they think, 'I been clean a year now, so maybe I can just smoke a blunt on the weekends.' But an addict can't *ever* control how much he's goin' to use. Not for long, anyways. We have to practice total abstinence. I've accepted that I cannot change that. Ever. That's why I'm still clean."

He paused to take a bite of his pancakes.

"Other people think they can change the rules of recovery," he continued. "They think, 'I don't need those AA meetings no more. I don't need the 12 steps. I can stay clean without them. Or 'I can still live with this person who's usin' every day right in my face; it won't make me go back.' And, of course, they end up usin'. *Every* time."

We ate for a while, and then he changed the subject. "So you know anything about where we goin'?"

"Not much. I've driven through Southeast many times...even did an interview down there on a previous case. But I've never seen the drug scene from the inside."

"Well, I want to prepare you. It's goin' to be bad. You're goin' to see some of the ugliest things a person can see," he said, deadly serious now.

"I'm not looking forward to it, but it needs to be done."

"Why? What are you tryin' to accomplish?"

"Didn't James tell you?" I asked.

"Yeah, but I want to hear it from you."

"I'm working for a woman whose son was murdered," I said. "The son was a good guy, just happened to be in the wrong place at the wrong time and got hit in a drive-by. She's hired me to find who did it. The only lead I've got is a cousin named Carla, whose been on the streets since since she was fourteen. I'm hoping that she heard something about who did it."

"That ain't much to go on. You sure you want to risk dyin' over something that flimsy?"

"I know it's weak, but I've got nothing else," I admitted.

"Hmmm," he muttered, leaning back in his chair. It creaked loudly. "Well, for starters, if there's one thing I've learned from a lifetime in the streets, it's that people ain't ever in the wrong place at the wrong time. That boy was in the life; he was dealin' or owed someone some money."

"That was my first thought, and I looked into it. I'm telling you there's no evidence of that. This guy was Mr. Clean."

He looked skeptical. "Well," he said, "another possibility was that he got smoked by someone doin' an initiation."

"A what?" I asked.

"A gang initiation. But in D.C. we don't call 'em gangs; we call 'em crews. When you join up, sometimes they ask you to kill someone on the street. Anyone. To prove that you a stone-cold killer and loyal enough to do anthing."

He paused to let that sink in and then said, "We'll head down there after breakfast. It's better to go in the daytime. I wouldn't even think of goin' at night. That's when most of the killin' happens."

We finished up breakfast and said our good-byes to Mother.

Then we walked out onto H Street and got into Sterling's beat-up '88 Sentra. As we pulled out into the traffic, he said, "First stop is a shooting gallery down by the Navy Yard."

"A shooting gallery? What is that?" I asked, knowing I wouldn't like the answer.

"It's an abandoned building that addicts use to shoot up heroin or smoke crack. Be careful where you step when we get inside. There'll be used needles and broken glass everywhere on the floor. A lot of the needles will have blood on them, and about half the heroin addicts in the city are HIV positive."

"Just great," I said, exhaling.

"Also, whatever happens, don't go in the building before me. I'll go in first, and let certain people know who you are and get permission for you to come in. If you don't wait, you're gonna get shot."

"No problem."

We drove past an endless number of rundown row houses and brown, decrepit three-and-four-story buildings. Every corner seemed to have a liquor store with a big lotto sign hanging in the window. Liquor and lotto; the fantasy fuel of the discontented. Fake hope for the hopeless.

People stood around on the corners, and occasionally I could see someone exchange money for drugs. It always happened quick—standing close together with a minimum of movement—like two kids surreptitiously passing a note in class.

Grandmothers walked kids down the streets past piles of trash and broken glass. The older generation trying to hold what's left together. A homeless man wandered down the street, shuffling beneath dignity. Everything was broken or ugly or dirty. There was a feeling that anything could happen to anyone at anytime.

Having spent my life living high up on a terrace of privilege, I realized that this was a reality I could look into, but never truly enter. I was like an anthropologist studying a foreign tribe—no matter how much I was here, I could never truly BE here. I could be *in* here, but not *of* here.

Eventually we parked on Wheeler Avenue in Congress Heights across the street from an abandoned apartment complex. It stretched the length of the block, and most of the windows were broken or boarded up. The strip of grass in front was growing unchecked. Trash was scattered around the curb and sidewalk. On a broken door was a sign that said: "Clean It or Lien It. The owner of this private property has been ordered to clean it. If not, the D.C. Government will clean the property and charge the owner twice the cost. D.C. Department of Public Works." Near a corner of the building was another sign that said: DRUG FREE ZONE. I wondered if the people who had hung that sign had seen the irony.

"I may be awhile; you can't rush this. Sit tight," Sterling said.

As he got out of the car, I saw his age in the way he had trouble straightening up. I felt a flash of guilt about asking him to do this.

"You sure you're ok with this?" I asked. "I don't want to put you into a situation like this if you've got reservations."

He smiled and asked, "Do you believe in karma?"

"Yeah. But not from one life to the next. I believe we answer for our mistakes in this life."

"I used heroin for most of my adult life," he said, leaning down to speak through the open car door. "I hurt my kids and nearly drove my wife insane. I hooked other people onto drugs. I've got a lot of bad stuff to make up for. That's why I want to help."

I nodded and said, "Fair enough."

He turned and made his way to the front door of the building, opened it without hesitation and walked in.

I sat in the car and stared at the building through the driver's side window. After a couple of minutes, I saw a woman walk hurriedly down the street. She was skeleton thin, wearing a dirty t-shirt, ragged shorts, and flip-flops. Her hair was all over the place, and there were marks like burns on her face that I couldn't identify. Her skin had a grayish pallor. She went through the same door as Sterling and disappeared into the darkness inside.

Later a couple of young boys walked by, tossing a football back and forth between them. As they passed, they looked at me warily with hundred-year-old eyes.

Finally Sterling returned and said, "All right. It took some talkin', but I convinced them that you wasn't 5.0. Let's go."

I jumped out of the car and walked towards the building behind Sterling, glad for the comforting feel of the .45 in it's quick-draw holster against my left side. I checked to make sure that it wasn't breaking the natural line of my jacket, then walked into hell.

As we weaved our way through dark hallways and rooms, people sat or lay against the walls everywhere. In the dim light, I saw a man lying unconscious in his own feces and vomit, a woman sticking a needle into an open wound in her arm, another woman sucking deeply on a crack pipe like it was a lovers cock, while an emaciated woman next to her sat staring into space with dead eyes and the same thousand-yard stare as the soldier in that famous painting. A lot of people seemed to have it, but they were a different kind of veteran— veterans of their own degradation. I saw a man reach into a glass of bloody water that was filled with used needles. Piles of trash, dirty bloody rags, and broken glass were everywhere. A place to make the soul waste away, sicken and die. I walked through it with a kind of uncomprehending numbness, my defense against horror; it was too surreal to wrap my mind around.

We entered a room in the rear of the building on the second floor. Three young men lounged in filthy chairs. Two had corn-rowed hair; the other's head was shaved. They all had a uniform of sorts; T-shirt with the arms cut off, expensive jewelry, and gang tattoos.

The one on the right cradled an AK-47. He lay his gun against the wall, got up, and came over to pat me down. He found the .45 and took it out of its holster. He held it up to examine it, then said, "Nice piece."

"Thanks."

"Yo, let me see it," one of the other boys said.

The guy standing next to me tossed the .45 to his friend, who deftly snatched it out of mid-air.

"Hmmm. This is nice. All we ever see is 9's. What is it?" he asked.

".45 caliber ACP."

He looked straight at me. "Maybe I'll keep it as payment for whatever we tell you."

"Oh, come on, Marcus," Sterling broke in gently. "This guy is a private eye. He ain't makin' money like you. Cut him some slack man."

Marcus looked me over. He was clearly the leader. I avoided direct eye contact, staring impassively at the wall just above his head. It served no purpose to escalate things—yet. But if it came to that, I had a back-up piece hidden in an ankle holster.

Finally Marcus said, "All right, Sterling. Only for you. I owe you, anyway. He'll get this back when we done. So what you want, white boy?"

"I'm looking for a woman named Carla Jones. Around thirty-five, five foot four," I told him.

"She a crack 'ho?"

"Yeah. She may shoot heroin, too."

The three guys looked at each other.

Marcus said, "Any of you know this 'ho?"

"Nah, bra', don' know dat bitch," the one next to me said.

"I used ta deal wit a Carla that used ta suck my dick for crack, but dat 'ho is only around nineteen or tweny," the other guy slurred.

Marcus turned to me and tossed my gun back, saying, "Don't know her. Looks like this ain't your lucky day. Now get the fuck outa' here. Sterling, my brother, you have a nice day."

Stepping into the sunlight again was a relief. Sterling visibly exhaled as the tension left his body.

As we settled into the car, I said, "I've seen some crazy shit in my life but ..." I shook my head in disbelief.

He turned and looked at me with sad eyes and nodded. "Yeah."

"That guy Marcus, ... he said he owes you?"

"I got his brother into treatment."

"But he still sells drugs?" I asked.

"Don't expect it to make no sense; it never has, and it never will."

Later as we drove through the city, Sterling said, "You did well in there. Kept your mouth shut at the right times and kept your cool. They like to mess with people, but they didn't mess with you much. I was surprised how easy it was to talk Marcus into givin' your gun back. I think it's cause they looked you over and decided that you was not easily trifled with."

"Hmmm."

"So what did you think of Marcus and his crew?" Sterling asked, looking over at me briefly, obviously curious to see an outsider's reaction.

"Scared kids who think that their survival lies in being scarier than the people who scare them. Salvageable if they felt like they had some other options in life."

He looked at me in surprise and said, "Yeah. That's it exactly."

"Really young," I added. "That one kid couldn't have been more than 16,"

"It's a young man's game. None of 'em live long enough to get old. If they do, it's 'cause they got locked up for life."

We drove in silence for a long while, until I asked, "When we first walked in, did you see the man reaching into that glass of bloody water for a needle? What was he doing?"

"He didn't have no works, so he was borrowin' the house works," Sterling said. "People come in all day and use the same needles. That's why most of the addicts in the city got HIV, Hepatitis, and all kinds a' otha things."

"Don't they know the risks?"

"Somewhere in the back of their minds, I think they know it. But it's so far back, they can't see it. When you in the life, you only think about three things: getting the money to get drugs, getting the drugs, and using them. Everything else—kids, job, health, pride—gets pushed outa' your head."

"So it becomes a total obsession," I said.

"Yeah."

I had more questions, but paused as Sterling negotiated a traffic snarl, swerving to avoid a couple of cars stopped in the right-hand lane, and just beating a bus going for his spot in the road.

When we were stopped at the next light, I asked, "What were those sores I saw on people's arms?"

"Those are abscesses. It's an infection that eats into your arm, or wherever on your body you're shootin' up. I used to have them. Look here, and you can see the scars." He held out his right arm for me to examine. It was covered with irregular scar tissue.

"That one woman was injecting heroin right into the abscess. Why, in God's name, would she do that?"

"You use long enough, and most of the veins in your arm will collapse. After that you get a hit wherever you can. In the feet, the groin, the neck, or forehead, even into an abscess."

"Unbelievable," I said, shaking my head.

"When you in the same place in your head as they are, it's not unbelievable. It's everyday life."

We found him in an alley just north of the Navy Yard. Leon J. Wright, known on the streets as "Blow." He was collapsed in a heap near the mouth of the alley, ass in a puddle of god knows what, head sunk downwards in a heavy dope nod. Two long lines of spittle hung from the corners of his mouth, coming to rest on a bushy, nappy beard, and the rags he wore were covered with stains and stink.

"Blow! Blow!" Sterling said, shaking his arm roughly, trying to rouse him from heroin dreams.

He took a slow, weak swat at Sterlings's hand and mumbled something incomprehensible, but his head did not come up.

"BLOW! Get up motherfucker!" Sterling yelled this time, shaking him harder.

No response. Sterling tried for another couple of minutes, then gave up.

"Damn," he said. "We got to wait till some of the dope wears off. He musta' just took a massive hit to be out like that."

"Can we wait somewhere else? It stinks in here."

"Nah, man. If he wakes up and leaves, and we miss him, he's goin' to be hard to find again."

"Shit." It was an exclamation and observation, as there was quite a bit laying about the alley. Probably from local dogs, but who knew.

Sterling leaned back against the nearest wall, but I stayed where I was. The only thing I wanted in contact with this sewer was the soles of my shoes. I tried to remember if I was caught up on my immunizations.

My nose had just begun to adjust to the smell, and boredom had begun to drift down when two young toughs pushed their way out of a decrepit door in the back of the alley. They paused, surprised to see us standing in their space. I glanced at Sterling. He looked scared.

"What the fuck is this!?" one of them said as they sauntered up to us.

They were in their early twenties, and had the confident, hungry look of predators.

"This," I said sharply, "is police business." I drew my .45, and gave them my best piercing stare. "And this," I said, waving the gun in Blow's direction, "is my suspect. Now back the fuck off, or I'll make *you* my business!"

To my surprise, they backed off without hesitation and went back through the door, slamming it closed behind them.

Sterling smiled broadly, clearly relieved. "I *told* you people would think you was a cop."

"Yeah, it wasn't hard to convince them."

"Way to go, man! We could a' been in some real trouble there. That door they came out of, it ain't a crack house. Not enough traffic in the alley for it to be a crack house. It's probably where they keep their supply, and do the mixin' and baggin'. That's death to invade that space."

We went back to waiting.

From deep within the recesses of his rags, we heard Blow humming to himself. I was surprised to recognize it—Miles Davis's Stella By Starlight. Odd that a guy like this would know it.

Sometime later, he raised his head and slowly looked around, eyelids still loose and heavy. "Sterling!" he drawled, "whas up brotha?!"

"What's up, Blow!" Sterling leaned down and took a closer look at him, then said mournfully, "Oh, man, look at what you've done to yourself! You was doin' good there for a while."

"What you talking about? I'm doin' fine," he said, scratching his head lazily. "Just a temporary set-back, is all."

"This is one hell of a set-back, brother. About a hundred miles back."

"Nah, nah. I'm goin' to get myself back up into treatment real soon. Maybe next week." His head dropped loosely backwards, hitting the wall behind him, and his eyes rolled up slightly into the back of his head.

"Yeah, right. Listen, we're trying to find a girl named Carla Jones. You know her?"

He looked at us both, focus slightly sharpened. "Who?" he said, buying time to think, to figure all the angles. I could tell he was already looking for a way to turn this into his next fix.

"Carla Jones. Around 35, light-skinned, been runnin' the streets for years."

"She suck that glass dick?"

"Yeah. She does horse, too."

"Maybe I do know her. How much you give me ta tell ya?"

"I ain't givin' you shit," Sterling said firmly. "It'll just go into your arm, and I ain't goin' to help you kill yourself."

"Ah, come on Sterling. I just need a couple billy's ta get me through the week. Till I gets up in treatment."

"Man, you forget who you talkin' to? I know all the lies, brother, cause I *told* all the lies. No way. That's not happinin'. I will buy you some food, though. Get a good warm meal up in you. I bet its been a while since that happened…."

Blow grumbled and mumbled, cursed, and complained, then finally accepted the offer.

"Sterling," I said. "There's no way we can get this guy into a restaurant. He looks like he hasn't bathed in a year."

"I know. We'll have to buy it and bring it to him. Find a bench where he can eat it."

There was no bench to be found, so we ended up sitting in Sterling's car, with the windows open to disperse the smell. Unfortunately, however, this guy had some world-class funk, so the open windows didn't to do much good. I took to breathing through my mouth.

"How'd you get the name Blow?" I asked him. We were in the back seat, waiting for Sterling to bring the food.

"Sterling didn't tell you?"

"No."

"I used to play with Dizzy."

"Are you shitting me? Dizzy Gillespie? *The* Dizzy Gillespie?"

He grinned broadly, exposing a row of missing teeth, obviously pleased with the effect of his revelation. It had probably been a long time since he had impressed anyone.

"Yeah, I toured with him back in '63. Best year of mah' life."

"What did you play?"

"Alto sax. That's how I got the name Blow."

He had me completely. Being a major jazz fanatic, it wasn't hard to do. I fired a thousand questions at him about his days with Dizzy, all which he answered gleefully, delighted to relive better days. Eventually, I asked him the question that had been on my mind since I first saw him.

"So what happened? How'd you end up like this?"

He didn't seem offended. Rather, the opposite. He reveled in the interest. "Ah, now, that's a story! It started when I was in the Army, back in '57, working in a medical supply warehouse, on a base in Tennessee. They had all these old morphine styrettes, surplus that'd been stored since World War Two. Boxes and boxes, stored to the sky! Dope fiend heaven!"

We paused as Sterling slid into the car and handed out burgers to everyone. Blow took a ravenous bite, then continued. "I fell in with this crooked supply Sergeant. He was selling the styrettes on the street and making huge amounts of cash. I helped him move the product and alter the inventories. One night, when we was bored, we decided to try it together. We had already been smoking weed, and were curious about this stuff that people seemed willing to do *anything* to get. We'd had white guys offer their girlfriends for it, their cars, their asses, *anything*. We figured, damn, this shit must be *good*. So, we did each other, a skin-pop into the arm, 'cause we didn't know anything about mainlinin' yet. And, goddamn, if that shit didn't hit me like a train! Knocked my ass right into heaven. I was flying for the next 5 hours. That was the day that I learned that there ain't nothin' like a shot a dope. A shot a dope is better than pussy, ain't it Sterling?!"

"At first it is. But the better the high, the higher the price," Sterling responded. "Besides," he said, turning to me, perhaps worried that Blow might give me ideas, "after a while your tolerance goes up and you can't shoot enough dope to get high. You're using to not feel sick. You're paying hundreds of dollars a day to feel normal. I get that for free now."

Blow shrugged that off, clearly not wanting to dwell on such unpleasant realities. *His* reality. "So, we went like that for about six months. Sellin' and usin' and getting monster habits. Then, one day, a guy who'd been using with us caught a bad batch of morphine and died. The base police started to investigate. Soon, we got word through a friend who worked in the base commanders office that they was going to arrest us the next morning, and ship us straight off to Leavenworth. That night, I packed my car with all the morphine I could get into it, drove off base, and never came back. I ended up in New York City. Lived in Greenwich, sold mainly to the musicians and artists, and eventually met Burroughs, who introduced me to Ginsburg and Kerouac. You know who they are?"

"Do I know who they are!? Of course, I was reading their stuff when I was sixteen."

"Yeah, well, I sold them Benzedrine inhalers. They was big back then. They were never into the dope. Except Burroughs. He was into it in a big way."

"So how'd you end up with Dizzy?" I asked.

"I'd played sax since I was a young boy, but let it go once I got into the dope. Then, one night, Kerouac took me down to Hell's Kitchen to hear Monk play. It straight out kicked my fucking ass. I started dealing him dope to get close to him. Shit, it wasn't hard, all the musicians did dope back then. I used to give him a good price and the occasional freebie. We'd shoot up and talk music. I soaked up everything that motherfucker ever said and started to play again, trying to get beyond technique like he had, and into pure improvisational freedom. I never got nearly as good as Monk, but I got good and eventually hooked up with Dizzy. I started having problems, though, on tour. I was separated from my supplier and having trouble getting my dope. I started spending a lot of hours in whatever city we was in chasing my next fix. Started missing practices, and then one night, missed a gig. Dizzy fired me on the spot. And that was the end of jazz for me. I spent the next 20 years in-and-out of jail, using, dealin', going through treatment programs. And here I am today, still doin' the same motherfuckin' thing."

"Don't have to be that way, Blow," Sterling said. "I could get you up into the 2nd and D Shelter today, and into the methadone program on K Street."

"Man, I been up in both those places before, and every other one. They ain't done nothin' for me!"

"That's cause you didn't let them. You got to surrender, take it one day at a time. It works if you work it, brother."

"Fuck that AA noise. I've surrendered all right. Surrendered to the fact that I was born a dope fiend and am going to die one."

That put a crimp in the conversation for a while, and we sat in silence, finishing our food. Blow was having trouble keeping it in his mouth—hard to do when you don't have any front teeth—and bits and pieces of gummed up bun and meat and ketchup fell into his beard and clothes.

Finally, Sterling said, "So, we had a deal. You got your meal, and now it's time to answer our question. You know Carla Jones?"

"Yeah, I know her. Nearly everyone knows Carla. She been on the streets forever. Ain't seen her in a while, though. Maybe a couple years. I know she used to hook over on MLK, back when it was the spot. Why you want to see her, anyway?"

"We want to know if she heard anything about her cousin's murder," I said.

"Shit, if you find Carla, she probably will. Fuck CNN, the streets is the best news source on the planet."

A street of rotting souls, of thinly-veiled desperation, of forced interest and faked desire. Martin Luther King Avenue. They hovered near the edge of the sidewalks, dead eyes scanning the passing cars, ready to sell their mouths and cunts and souls for twenty dollars.

We wandered northward, chatting the girls up as we went, asking for information about Carla. It always played out the same. Our approach would elicit a barrage of tired offers, disguised in oblique language that was designed to avoid arrest.

"You lookin' for a date?"

"You want some company, baby?"

"Oh, you hot, honey! I'll give you a real good time."

J.D. Miller

Then came our denial and questions about Carla, which they dismissed with a wave of the hand, a grimace, or obscenity as they turned back towards the streets. Anyone not a customer was dead to them.

The only variation in the theme was a male crossdresser, who had a bad case of verbal diarrhea, and did good business with gay men in denial. They wanted to have sex with a man, and be able to tell themselves that it doesn't really count because he's dressed like a woman. Anyway, that's what he/she told us, including other gems, such as:

"Behind every good man is …. another man, doin' him just right."

"I can toss a salad like Martha Stewart." He wasn't talking about cooking.

"Oh, lord, I need to paint my toenails. Look at them, all chipped."

"Child, am I a queen or what? If I went to Disneyland, Tinker Bell would have to move over!"

Finally, he stopped long enough for us to fire a question about Carla.

He responded, "Oh, yeah, I remember that skanky bitch. Never could stand her. You need to talk to Renee, she used to hang with Carla. She's usually on the corner a couple blocks down."

When we got to the corner, we saw a small girl, with fine, delicate features, dressed in a micro-mini. She was like a little broken bird, with the saddest eyes, the kind that arouse all of man's protective instincts. I wanted to save her, to shove her in Sterling's car and take her away from all this. But, another part of me knew better. She wouldn't be out here if she wasn't damaged beyond my ability to help her. She was probably addicted to drugs, hooking to support her habit, and in love with some abusive, scumbag boyfriend, who she would refuse to leave.

"You Renee?" Sterling asked her.

"No. I'm Stephanie. Who are you? You cops?" she asked.

"No, we're not," I said. "I'm a private investigator. We want to ask Renee a few questions about Carla Jones. Word is she used to hook out here a couple of years ago."

"I never heard of her. But Renee should be back soon. She got picked up a couple of minutes ago. It never takes more than ten or fifteen minutes."

"We'll wait," I said.

There was an awkward silence for a minute, which Sterling broke by asking, "What's a sweet little thing like you doin' out here? You could do better than this."

"Fuck you! I'm doing fine," she snapped violently. So much for the broken little bird theory. "Why don't you two fuck off! As long as you're standing here, no one's going to stop and pick me up. Stevie!" she called out to some unseen person.

A guy stepped out from around the corner and walked towards us. White, early thirties, with a cocky air.

"What the fuck is going on here?!" he said. This was probably the scumbug boyfriend—pimp really— and now we were going to get the *'look how intimidating I am'* act. He stepped up close to us, flipped open his jacket, and put his hand on the butt of a gun that was stuck into his waistband. I could tell he wasn't going to draw, he just wanted to show us that he was carrying.

I'd had it. The tension and disgust had been building all day, and I put it all into an explosive right undercut that lifted him off his feet, bounced him off a wall and onto the ground, out cold. Stephanie gave a little squeal, but didn't move. Sterling stared at me wide-eyed.

I stepped over to him, reached down, yanked out the pistol, and threw it into some bushes.

Stephanie was looking at her man, lying face-down on the pavement, with a strange combination of satisfaction and despair. The part of her that knew he was a scumbag who leeched off the misery of others was happy to see him get whacked. But the sick part of her that loved him in spite of that was saddened to see him hurt. She stood silent for a long time, paralyzed by the opposing forces working within her.

Sterling looked at me closely for a moment, trying to see if I was calmed down enough to reason with. Then he pulled me off to the side, and began speaking to me in a hushed voice. "Man, I understand why you did this, but it was a big mistake. You just made him look like a chump in front of his woman and all the other ho's around here. When he wakes up, the only way he's going to be able to get his respect back is to wail on a couple people, and it ain't goin' to be you or me. He's goin' to take it out on his girls. They probably goin' to get beat real bad."

"Shit! So what should I do?"

"Man, I don't know. Just don't do it again."

I thought for a moment then walked over to Stephanie. She reeled back slightly, clearly afraid of me now. "It's ok," I said, holding my hands up, palms outward, to reassure her. "I just want to talk to you.

Sterling tells me that your boyfriend is going to take this out on you when he wakes up. If that's so, I'm sorry. Is there anything I can do to help? You want me to stick around and scare him worse? Call the police? Take you somewhere?"

Her face instantly twisted into an expression of disgust, as if my concern for her was a sign of weakness. Damn! This was one sick, twisted fuck.

"I can handle him," she said, sneering. "I'll tell him some fucking lie that will fool him. Men are *always* easy to fool. I'll tell him you ran off scared of what he'd do when he woke up, or that you heard of his rep' and freaked. So if you want to help me, do it by *FUCKING OFF* before he wakes up!"

Just then, a battered white sedan slid to a stop in front of us, the passenger side door flew open, and out came a chubby woman with mocha colored skin who was, for some reason, wearing a heavy winter coat in spring. She slammed the door shut without looking backwards, and her john pulled away quickly. She took in the scene at a glance—Stephanie looking at me angrily, her boyfriend face-down on the sidewalk, and froze. She said, "Oh, shit! What's going on here? Stephanie, are they cops?!"

"No," she said, "just a couple of jerk-offs looking for you."

"Hey, Stephanie," I said, "whatever you're on….up the dosage, cause it ain't working."

Sterling put a calming hand on my shoulder, smiled at me, then turned to Renee and said, "Hi. My name is Sterling, and this is Mark Christian. We want to ask you some questions about Carla Jones."

"Why? Did something happen to her?"

"No. Not that we know of. We're just trying to find her. Mr. Christian here is a private investigator, and has been hired by Carla's family to see if she's ok."

It was a lie, but had a better chance of working than the truth, so I went with it.

"I know where she is, but if you want me to tell you, you got to pay for it."

Sterling sighed and said to me, "That's the streets for you. Everyone is always trying to get over."

"We all got to make a living," Renee said.

"And get our next fix," Sterling countered.

"Yeah. But before we do business, let's get outa here," she said, pointing towards Stephanie's boyfriend. "If he wakes up, you're going to have to kill him."

"That would be easy enough," I said. "But I'd prefer not to. Let's go."

We were two blocks down the street when we heard a voice behind us screaming, *"You are dead, motherfuckers! You hear me! Dead! Me and my crew are going to come at you like the Gotti boys! Cut your fucking heads off, motherfucker!"*

"I guess he woke up," I said to Sterling.

"Yeah," Sterling said, glancing nervously over his shoulder. I didn't bother. After a lifetime of confrontations, I could tell the difference between a dog that's just barking, and one that's going to bite.

Two blocks later we were in Sterling's car and heading east through sparse traffic.

"Will you guys drop me off on Bladensburg Road? I don't want to go back to MLK for a couple of days. Not till Stevie calms down."

"Sure," Sterling said.

"Great. Now let's talk business. The information you want will cost you two hundred dollars."

Sterling laughed. "Two hundred dollars! You sell that thing between your legs for twenty!"

"Fifty, bitch. I ain't no cheap ho'."

"Fine, then. I'll pay you that," I said, feeling increasingly impatient. I knew that Sterling would disapprove, given that the money would probably go to drugs, but I was goddamned if I was going to sit through another lunch. "Where is Carla?"

"I ain't seen her in a couple years, but last I heard she was hanging out at Langston Place, working for one of the dealers there. I don't know who."

Sterling said, "Shouldn't be too hard to find out. I know someone over there we can talk to."

Just before we dropped Renee off, she said, "Gimme another twenty and I'll give you a blowjob. Thirty five for the both of you."

It was the easiest 'no' I ever said in my life.

At Langston Place Southeast, we parked across from a long line of cars queued up for service from the corner drug dealers. The majority of people in the cars were white and ran the economic spectrum. Just ahead of us was a couple of nervous looking teenagers in Daddy's SUV. In front of them was an aging white guy in a beat up old sedan, clearly working class.

Sterling saw my surprise and said, "White folks comin' in from the suburbs. A lot of the money that fuels the drug trade comes from them. The only difference between these folk and the ones you saw in the shooting gallery is that they got more money, more choices in life, and they can drive out of all this after they cop their drugs. So the bottom ain't as low for

79

them as it is for us here. You should see it on a Friday or Saturday night when all the young white kids are in town to party. The line is twice as long."

"No kidding."

"Yeah. And that ain't all. The dealers down here usually buy their guns from white gun dealers in Maryland or Virginia. They might be fourteen, but they can get just about anything from 'em, AK's, Armalite's, the works. After all, who cares when it's black folks. Give 'em the guns and let 'em kill each other, right," he said, his face tight. It was the first time I had seen him angry.

"It's like them school shootin's," he said. "I been amazed at the amount of ruckus on TV. All the sudden the reporters are concerned about the 'epidemic of violence.' Shiiit. Ain't nobody noticed the violence till white kids started to die."

He paused to take a breath, visibly trying to calm himself. "We always got a choice though. No matter how much we're discriminated against, we still got a choice to do right or wrong."

"Yeah," I said, "but that's used against you sometimes, too, isn't it? People use that as an excuse to blame the victim."

He looked at me again in surprise. "You know, when I first met you I thought maybe you was just a dumb gym bunny. It's nice to see you got a brain to match the body."

"Um, thanks."

I followed his lead as he got out of the car and crossed the street. I watched as one car in the buy line pulled away, and another pulled up. A dealer stepped on either side of the car that had pulled up. One did the actual transaction, while the other looked into the car menacingly.

We walked past them and made our way to a young guy sitting on a park bench about fifteen feet from the street, in a good location to observe the action. He looked about nineteen, with a strong face and slender body. He was dressed in expensive sweats, and his head was shaved bald. The sweats bulged on the left side where he had a pistol tucked into his waistband. His face brightened when he saw Sterling.

They clasped hands, and Sterling introduced us. "Kenny, this is Mr. Christian. He's a private investigator. Like on TV."

"No shit," he said. "Like *Magnum PI* and shit?"

"Yeah," I said, smiling. "That's me."

"Kenny, we lookin' for a girl named Carla Jones," Sterling said.

"Sure, I know Carla. She used to buy from me a couple years ago. I heard she's workin' as a look-out for Tommy E. now."

"Ah, shit," Sterling said. His face was pinched with concern.

"Ah, shit is right," echoed Kenny.

"Who is he?" I asked, trying to figure what had Sterling so spooked.

Kenny looked at me like the ignorant outsider I was and said, "You ain't never heard a Tommy E.? He run the SD crew outa' Stanton Apartments on 15th Street. That boy put away more people than all the other dealers in the city put together. Hell, I might be next. Hey, Sterling, if I get capped, you gonna come to my funeral? I got it all planned, bro....it's gonna be real nice."

J.D. Miller

I studied his face, looking for a sign that he was kidding. There was none.

"Yeah, Kenny, I'll come," Sterling said sadly. "But you get outa the life, and maybe you won't have to die."

"And do what? Work at McDonalds? Shiiit! I can't support my momma and sisters and kids on that kinda change."

"No disrespect, bro," Sterling responded quickly, "but you ain't goin' to be able to support them when you're dead either."

We said our goodbyes to Kenny and thanked him for the information, then went back to the car. Once inside, Sterling said, "There's another problem that I didn't want to talk about in front of Kenny. I owe Tommy E. some money, and he's got a long memory. I go with you to see him, and I'm dead."

"I understand. No problem. I'll go on my own."

Sterling looked a bit guilty and began to explain. "Just before I cleaned up, I was dealin' to support my habit. Tommy E. was on the way up, and he fronted me some drugs—a lot of drugs—to sell on the street. We was supposed to split the profits after I sold them. But I was in a bad way back then, shootin' up eight and nine times a day, and havin' those drugs in my pocket was like givin' a starvin' man a plate of food. I mean, they was _burnin'_ a hole in my pocket. So the first thing I did is go back to this little alley, pull out a packet or two or three of the drugs Tommy had just givin' me, and shoot up. I liked the first hit so much that I kept on goin' until I passed out. I don't know how long I was out, but when I woke up, the drugs was gone, along with my jacket, wallet, and shoes. Some motherfucker

82

cleaned me out. I knew there wouldn't be no explaining to Tommy; when he found out, he'd shoot me on sight. So I went into a treatment center to hide from him. I figured that was the one place he wouldn't look for me. So my motives for gettin' treatment weren't too noble. But you know, somehow I wised up while I was in there, and here I am today."

"Damn," I said. "You haven't had a boring life, have you?"

"No, I haven't."

"Well, Sterling, I appreciate everything you've done. I wouldn't have gotten this far without you," I said sincerely. "And I'm starting to appreciate the risks you've taken to help me. I'm sure Tommy E.'s boys leave their neighborhood on occasion. If one of them had seen you driving around..."

"Yeah. We'd be dodging bullets."

Sterling drove me back to my motorcycle, which was still parked in front of Mother's restaurant. Maybe it was too crappy to steal. As I got out of Sterling's car, I gave him my number and told him to give me a call if he ever needed anything.

He said, "That boy who died—Eric. Tell his momma that even if you never find who killed him, life will take care of business. Them dealers always end up dead or locked up for life. *Always.* Whoever did this will get nailed eventually. The bill is in the mail."

"Yeah, and I'm going to deliver it."

-9-

I was wakened the next morning by the glow of sunlight coming through the window, bright enough to fire the inside of my closed eyelids a brilliant red. Lazily I turned over, hoping to get away from the light and back to sleep, but as I moved, the sharp squeak of the bed springs woke me further. Slowly ascending to full consciousness, I was blissfully aware of the silence of the mountains after a couple of days in the city. No cars rushing by, buses squealing to a stop, honking, or sirens. Not a damn thing except the chorus of birds softly singing in the woods outside my window.

Eventually I swung into a sitting position on the bed, then glanced at the alarm clock perched precariously on a pile of books. It said 6:45. Shit, I hadn't been up this early since the I was in the Corps. I reminded myself that I needed to quit smoking soon, then lit a cigarette.

The early spring light came through the east window in solid bands of whitish yellow, broken by the softly swirling shadows of smoke that drifted off my cigarette.

Rachel lay near the front door, her tail thumping gently against the rough wood floor. I beckoned, and she jumped on the bed, curling up beside me with her head on my lap. I rubbed her tummy while I smoked, thinking about the last couple of days and those coming. I was looking forward to the next couple of days off. Once the the cig was down to a nub, I stubbed it out in an ashtray, stood up and stretched, then let Rachel out to do her thing.

I stood on the porch for a minute taking in the panoramic view. When I'm home for long stretches of time, it disappears from notice, but after a couple of days away, I can see it with a fresh eye. It was like a Cole painting come to life. There was mist in the valley, making the surrounding hills look like islands in a white sea. Sunlight fired down in brilliant shafts through breaks in the low gray ceiling of clouds, spotlighting my mountain and turning a patch of mist to the west into a glowing sheet of shimmering yellow. Thoreau had written, "In a pleasant spring morning, all men's sins are forgiven. Such a day is a truce to vice." Today was such a day, I thought, gazing out in marvel at this amazing place that had become my home.

Eventually I went inside, made a pot of Kenyan coffee, and checked my mail. Most of it was junk, but one envelope caught my eye. I ripped it open, and inside was a check for $2000 from a previous client. I breathed a sigh of relief, since the money from Lillian Jones was not coming close to paying my bills. She didn't have much, so I was practically working pro bono.

The guy who sent me the check was named Joseph Kalinsky. I had met him a week before Lillian Jones. He was divorced two years prior. He had a court-ordered visitation schedule, but his wife had run off with their kid six months after the divorce. He had reported them missing to the police, but they had not been able to find them. When I told Joseph that I needed a non-refundable $1000 retainer, with an additional $2000 to be paid only if I found his son, he had huffed about finances and walked out. He came back and hired me the next day after checking with some other PI's, who had quoted prices in the $10,000 range.

I asked him where his ex-wife's relatives and close friends lived. Was there any state that she had dreamed about moving too? What was her religion? What grade would the kid be in this year? Did she have a drivers license? A lover? Did he know her social security number, and so on and so forth. Then I had escorted him out of the office and started to make some calls.

The first call was to a friend at the local sheriff's office. I asked him to run my client's name through the computer to see if he had ever been arrested for domestic violence or stalking. Obviously, I didn't want to find a wife and kid who had run away to escape abuse. Still, it never ceased to amaze me how many of my colleagues didn't care and never checked. Joseph came up clean.

When someone runs away, they usually go to live near someone they know, so I started calling the DMV's in states where his ex-wife's relatives and friends lived. Most DMV's will give you addresses for a modest fee, charged to a credit card when the transaction is done by phone. At each DMV, I asked for the ex-wife by her maiden name. I struck out five times until I called the Georgia DMV, and the clerk said, "I show a Donna Martin living at 49 Marlton Street, Alexis, Georgia, 09421.

"Do you have a phone number for her? She's an old high school sweetheart, who I'd like to say hi to."

"Sure," the female clerk said, giving me the number. "Good luck." I could hear the smile in her voice.

I called the number, and a little boy answered.

"Is this Jesse Martin?" I asked.

He replied *yes*, and I hung up.

I looked at my watch. It had taken forty minutes to find him. I called my client at his home number in Winchester, Virginia. It was about an hour's drive from my office, and he hadn't gotten home yet. I left a short message on his answering machine, telling him that I had found his ex-wife and son, and the address and phone number where he could reach them. Twenty-five minutes later he called me.

"I can't believe it! You found him in less than an hour! The police have been looking for over a year, and you do it while I'm driving home. It's a fucking miracle!!"

I thanked him, but felt like a fake. I had only done some common sense, routine things that the police usually don't have the time or motivation to do. Clients often attributed it to some magical, mystical process, but it was really just making the right calls and a little luck.

I encouraged him not to go rushing down there, to get a lawyer first, and do some planning. If he showed up unexpectedly, his ex might take off again. He thanked me and said that he would put a check for $2000 in the mail. Obviously, he had not put it in the mail immediately since it was three weeks later. But at least it was finally here in hand.

I did my workout in under an hour, showered, threw on some clothes, then jumped on my Triumph, and drove down the mountain to Flint Hill, where I deposited the money in the local bank.

I bought some grocery's at the town store. It didn't take long as there were only two aisles of food to choose from.

As I loaded the groceries into the carrier on the back of my bike, I had a chat with a couple of old guys playing chess in a shady spot just outside the store. They had lived in town forever and were like a living museum of Norman Rockwell's America. One even had the overalls and John Deere hat slightly tilted to the side. After a ten-minute discussion of the weather—living in the same town for seventy years tended to limit the breadth of one's conversation—I made a graceful exit.

I soared out of town, loving the wind against my face and the dappled shadows of sunlight shining through the leaves. The sky had cleared, and just a couple of clouds wandered above aimlessly.

As I turned to go up the mountain, I saw my neighbor, Bill Hunsaker, in his corral, working one of his new horses. He motioned for me to stop. I made a U turn and parked next to the corral.

He let go of the reins of the horse he was training, and came over, reaching out to shake my hand. His dirty work gloves felt rough against my skin as we shook. "Is everything ok?" he asked, a concerned look on his face.

"Sure, why do you ask?"

"A preacher just came by lookin' for you. We were afraid that maybe somebody had passed away in your family or something."

I laughed. "No, that's my best friend Greg. He's come out to stay for a couple of days."

His face brightened. "Oh, good. By the way, you talked to old Frank lately?" Frank was a quiet, grizzled old Korean war vet, who lived on the other side of the mountain.

"No. I've never met him."

"He's seen a couple of bears on the mountain," he said. "Little fellers, nothing to worry about. But you just might want to keep an eye on Rachel. You know how them dogs can get when a bear comes near the house."

"No, I don't."

"Well," Bill said, "most of the time they just get out of the way and maybe bark a bit. But now and then, they try to play the hero and scare the bear off the property, get too close, and get themselves a face full of bear claw. All it takes is one hit to kill a dog."

"Shit."

"Yeah," he said. "By the way, we haven't seen you in a couple of days. Where have you been?"

"In D.C. working on a new case."

"Well, I'm sure Alicia will be up soon to pester you. That girl's got a big thing for you."

I nodded, not knowing what to say.

He looked at me with an eyebrow raised and said half jokingly, "Now don't let me hear about you and my girl doing something. I'll have to come up there and clean house!" He laughed and slapped me genially on the back. He was a strong man, and my back went numb where he hit it.

"No, sir. Never happen. But is it ok if I do something with your wife?"

He laughed. "Now her, you can have!"

There was a black sedan parked next to my house. Greg must have checked it out of the parish car pool for the weekend. The Catholic church takes care of all a priest's material needs—food, clothing, car, living space, spending money—a small compensation for spending your life without the joy of romance and intimacy.

"Greg!" I yelled, jumping off my motorcycle and heading towards the house.

He opened the front door and peeked out, his face split by a grin. I leapt up on the porch, and we hugged. As always, I was overjoyed to see him. I leaned back, my hands on his shoulders, and we looked each other over. He was a little thinner, his face glowing with good health. A nose curved like an eagles beak, and big brown eyes that emanated intelligence, compassion, and love to the world.

"You need to work out, get those arms pumped up a bit more," he said with sarcastic good humor, motioning towards the muscles of my upper arm.

"I'll get right on it. Man, it's great to see you! I can't believe I finally got you out here."

"Yes," he said. "You know I'm a city boy; animals make me nervous."

"You ain't seen nothing yet. I just heard there's a bear on the mountain."

He looked genuinely concerned, and I could tell I was going to have a good time the next couple of days just goofing on his reactions. We were so totally accepting of each other that we could have fun teasing, and there was usually plenty of material because we both knew each other's eccentricities so well. But it was always done in a loving way, and neither of us had taken offense to the other in years.

We had met at the age of sixteen in a small-town Catholic Seminary in northwest Pennsylvania, on the southern bank of Lake Erie. The first day I met Greg, he was being mercilessly harassed by some classmates. He was the only black student in the Seminary and took a lot of shit for it. He was, however, a pacifist and refused to raise his voice or fist in self-defense. There was no fear, only a kind of sadness in his eyes as they picked him up to carry him outside and dump him in the snow.

One of the bastards made the comment, "Maybe some of the white will rub off on you, nigger."

I told them to put him down, and when they didn't, I hit the boy nearest me with a haymaker that put him out cold. The others backed off, and it was understood from that day on that Greg was under my protection, and no one ever messed with him again.

Greg was grateful, but talked to me about the ultimate futility of violence. Hate can only be overcome by love, he told me that first night of our friendship.

I thought *Jeez, man, I just saved your ass and I get a lecture*, but I was intrigued, as I had never met anyone as principled and decent.

As I got to know him better over the years, that impression had only deepened. He was deeply compassionate and intensely spiritual, but was not controlling or preachy about it most of the time. He was a bit monastic and very correct, but could still relax and laugh and have fun. His parishioners adored him and looked at him with the quiet worship that he so often inspired.

I put the groceries away and then broke out some chardonnay from a local vineyard and PG #5 cigars that I had been saving. We planted ourselves on the front porch and talked the rest of the day away.

We listened to Miles Davis's "Kind of Blue," and Pat Metheny's "Still Life (Talking)." We sang along badly to Van Morrison's "No Guru, No Method, No Teacher" and other favorite songs and cracked up at the hash we made of it.

"Now I've been all around the world, marching to the beat of a different drum, and maybe I've started to realize, baby the best is yet to come."

Greg marveled at a cottontail sniffing about the edge of the property, the cloud of daisies surrounding the house, and at the hawks circling overhead.

We talked and talked until the sunset crowning the surrounding peaks faded, and the moonlight slanted through the trees, making a silvery pattern on the spruce and pine needles that carpeted the floor of the forest. Overhead, a hundred million stars flickered and glowed brightly, incongruous in their interminable gaiety with the sullen wind that came through the valley. The lights from the farms and homes in Flint Hill were visible in the valley to the north, shining like some miniature galaxy at the bottom of a black sea.

We talked about everything; money, sex, love, friendship, the challenges of personal growth, the minutia of our daily lives. We talked about things that we had discussed a thousand times before, but always seemed fresh and exciting when shared with each other.

We decided that wealth was an empty goal, but was ok if it came as a side-effect of doing what you love. That most personal growth came from cultivating inner freedom, but that removing internal blocks to growth was a difficult process because they were so often unconscious and rooted in fear.

I kept quiet during the discussion of sex, not wanting to torture my celibate friend with glorious details. He spilled his ongoing struggle with celibacy, which had recently manifested itself somatically via a temporary paralysis of his left leg that no doctor could find a physical reason for. I did offer my opinion that the Catholic church needed to drop it's long-standing support of celibacy, which was profoundly unhealthy for its priests and often led to depression, alcoholism, gluttony, and child abuse.

He agreed somewhat but also saw the spiritual challenge in it and intended to rise to it fully. To him, it was the ultimate test of one's devotion to God. We also decided that relationships were best understood as bank accounts, that each word or action was a deposit or withdrawal that could consequently make it emotionally rich or bankrupt.

At one point Greg said, "I had a dream the other night that I wanted to tell you about. I was in my parish saying Mass. The pews were full, and you were sitting in the back row. There was a crashing sound, and the floor split open, and some sort of demonic beast rose from the earth screaming, and began to slaughter the people in the pews. You leapt forward to defend them, and it pushed you aside easily. I then stepped forward and began to pray to God for the protection of the people, and it reached out and threw me down too. I felt this horror and awful sense of powerlessness as it went on killing my parishioners. Then the dream ended."

"Intense. Do you think it means something?"

"I've thought a lot about it," he said. "You know that I'm not one to give cosmic significance to every dream I have. Often times they seem to be nonsense. But this one is different. Here's what I think. In the dream you and I represent different archetypes of the protector, the ideal of who we both strive to be. You guard their bodies, and I guard their souls. We can't help them because the demon is actually their own worst impulses, and ultimately neither of us have the power to save people from themselves. In a universe that operates on free will, we will never have that kind of power, nor should we want it. The dream is a call to humility. And, of course, the same is true for us; no one else can save us from our worst impulses or can force us to grow. Ultimately, each person is responsible for his own fate."

Finally, at about three a.m., we drifted off to sleep. Greg slept in my bed, and I stretched out in a sleeping bag on the floor.

The next morning was glorious, the skies a pristine cobalt blue. I set out to go fishing, leaving Greg on the porch hunched happily over a pad of paper, scribbling furiously, closing in on the finish to his first book on spirituality. He barely looked up as I said, "Bye," and walked into the woods.

I weaved my way down a trail that went around the mountain, overgrown and barely discernable, my fishing gear held loosely in hand. Rachel ranged in circles around me, eagerly chasing a rainbow of scents, breaking off only when she passed some invisible line that she sensed as being too far from me.

The forest that carpeted the mountain also covered ninety-five percent of the Blue Ridge, stretching hundreds of miles south into North Carolina and the Smoky Mountains. It was rich with five kinds of oaks (red, white, chestnut, scarlet, and black), three hickories (shagbark, pignut, and mockernut) and a variety of Virginia pine. It was also home to all sorts of rodents, rabbits, rattlesnakes, bobcats, owls, deer, squirrels, and the occasional bear.

After walking an hour, I stopped to rest in a meadow, lying on my back with Rachel next to me, skin warmed by sun, inhaling the rich scent of pine and clover. I smiled, as it seemed like the kind of place where one of Tolkien's hobbits could come wandering by, smoking a pipe and wondering why one of the "big people" was here. In my fantasy he sits down and shares the pipe, asking for news from far-away lands. What I'd seen in D.C. the last couple of days would probably scare him more than any tale of Sauron.

With that unwelcome thought I was up and moving again, striding for another half hour until I came to a river, sparkling in the sun. I waded in to mid-calf and made my first cast.

Rachel sat on the bank and stared at me curiously, her head tilted slightly, then gave up trying to figure out what I was doing, and lay down for a nap.

I watched the eddies and swirls of the river, the shadows beneath the scattered boulders and overhanging trees, trying to figure where the fish were.

Three more casts and I had one, reeling her in easily. It was a greenish, mid-size trout, wiggling furiously to protest its fate. I put it in the basket on the bank and kept on fishing until I had four.

When the sun began to slant down a good way behind the trees, I headed home, content as I had ever been.

That evening Greg and I sat down to eat the trout, took a bite, and rolled our eyes to heaven. Unbelievable. Delicious. After dinner, we called our old friends from the seminary and then crashed early, both exhausted from the little sleep we had gotten the night before.

I awoke the next morning to a scream. I bolted up in the bed and saw Greg dive through the front door, slam it behind him, and wedge a chair against it.

"There's a bear on the porch!!"

"What?"

"There's a bear on the porch! I got up to go outside, and it was sitting there looking at me!" Greg blabbered, his eyes wild with fear.

Rachel was hiding under the kitchen table. My house was one large room and a bathroom so I could see her a few feet from the bed, her ears flat against her head, softly whimpering.

A large, furry brown head rose in the side window and pressed it's wet nose against the screen, snuffling.

"There it is," Greg exclaimed loudly, pointing at the window while backing away. "Can it get through the window?"

"I don't know," I said laughing. "I think it's the fish. It's attracted to the smell of the fish."

I reached into the garbage, pulled out the remains of the fish, and put them in a bucket. I cautiously opened the front door, ignoring Greg's pleadings to keep it closed, and heaved the fish out into the front yard. I watched through the front window as the bear happily feasted, then wandered away into the woods.

I made some coffee and invited Greg to sit on the porch and chat before he had to leave. I knew that he had some pastoral counseling appointments and needed to get back to his parish today.

"I'm not leaving this cabin again," he said. "The only time I'm going to leave is to run to my car and get back to civilization."

-10-

I had no grand plan for meeting Tommy E. I was just going to keep it simple; walk up to his house and ask to see him, hoping that curiosity alone would get me inside. But first, I had to find out where he lived. I needed to talk to someone in the "know." Contacts in the right agencies are a priceless source of information, and I had quite a few.

I called "Butch" De Carlo, an old friend from the Marines who worked with the Drug Enforcement Administration (DEA). Butch and I had gone through Recon training together. Recon is to the Marines what the Green Berets is to the Army, a Special Forces group capable of operating behind enemy lines and reaching objectives via land, air, and sea. Of our class of seventy-three people, only nineteen made it through the training, including Butch and I. After Butch's brother died of a cocaine overdose, he had left the Marines to join the DEA. He'd been making drug dealers pay ever since.

After two rings, a bureaucratic office-type answered the phone and said in a smooth, robotic voice, "Mr. De Carlo is unavailable. He is in a meeting. May I have him call you back?"

I didn't respond. There were muted office sounds in the background; phones ringing, people talking and clacking away on keyboards.

"Hello? Are you there?"

"Oh, sorry, I was waiting for the beep," I said.

"Very funny."

I left a message, and Butch called me back an hour later.

When I made my request, he said loudly in a tone of complete disbelief, "You want to talk to who?! Have you lost your mind?"

"Nope. Same mind, same old me," I said, smiling.

There was a pause, and then he said, "I forgot; it is the same old you. You were a crazy bastard in the Corps, too."

"Aw, shucks, stop it. You're making me blush."

"Why the hell do you want to talk to Tommy E.?" he asked. "You looking for a new line of work? Not making enough as a private dick?"

"That's it. I'm switching to the dark side of the force. How come you DEA types are always so suspicious?"

"'Cause we deal with the worst in human nature."

"And I don't?"

"You got a point there," he said.

"By the way, how's married life?" I asked. I had been a groomsman in his wedding.

"Fair. I get bitched at a lot for working too much. Hey, when the fuck are you going to get off the fence and pick a partner?" he asked over the sound of his office mates chatting in the background.

I laughed. "No time soon."

"You're missing out, buddy. Joking aside, it's nice to have somebody steady."

"I'm on the Warren Beatty plan: marriage around fifty or so."

"God, your poor girlfriends," he sighed.

"Girlfriend. Singular."

"No shit? Still a serial monogamist?" he asked.

"Yup. Her name's Aislinn."

"Aislinn? What kind of name is that?"

"I think it's Celtic. Her parents are first-generation Irish immigrants," I said.

"Really. Thank God. For a minute I thought it might be one of those hippie names like Moonglow or Highbeam."

I laughed again. "No. She works at the Commerce Department."

"Oh. Definitely not a hippie type then."

"No. So how about it? Can you get me Tommy E.'s address?" I asked, changing the subject back to the reason for the call.

"Yes. But be careful," Butch said, sounding genuinely concerned. "This guy is a card-carrying psychopath. Smart. A natural leader and absolutely no conscience. He climbed all the way up from the bottom, and left a lot of bodies along the way."

"Think you'll be able to arrest him any time soon?" I asked.

"No. It's going to be a while. But he's definitely high on our list of people to get. Right now he's the biggest dealer in D.C. He's responsible for a lot of bad things, but hasn't done them himself for years. He always has his crew take the risks. And they're too afraid to talk when they get arrested. Talking would be a guaranteed death sentence."

There was a pause while I digested this latest clump of reassuring information.

"There's something else I meant to ask you. Why does everyone call him Tommy E.? What does the E. stand for?"

"The E stands for Easy, his nickname early in his career," Butch said. "Rumor has it when he was a teenager and did his first killing, some of the older guys in his crew asked him how it felt to kill someone. He said it was easy."

-11-

Tommy E. had made it out of the inner city and now lived in a mansion in Montgomery County. This was my third day of standing in front of the eight-foot tall, closed metal gate that led into his estate. It was one of those gates that scream, "Stay out!"

On the first day I had stood in front of the gate for about four hours, repeatedly buzzing the house on the intercom next to the gate, hoping to annoy someone into letting me in. No luck. At first, they politely told me to go away and then stopped responding.

On the second day they sent some people to follow me home in a red Mercedes, undoubtedly to beat the crap out of me, but I lost them easily. When tailing, never use a red Mercedes.

This was the third day, and I was starting to get pissed off. I was getting into that mansion today, whatever it took. It was either that or my investigation into the death of Eric Jones was probably over. Hell, maybe it was already over and I was just fooling myself, but I had to try.

Beyond the security gate, whose every contour and crack I had memorized by now, was a driveway curving up to Tommy's colonial-style mansion. The house was boxy, with four columns on the two-story front porch; traditional American architecture and nice camouflage. No one would suspect that this was the house of a major drug lord. It had an immaculate sloping lawn, but hedges that were sloppy and grown over. Having someone cut the lawn was probably the extent of Tommy's interest in landscaping.

On either side of the fence, security cameras were mounted on the brick wall that enclosed the property. They stared at me ominously. I waved just to be friendly and because I was easily entertained after three days of this shit.

Then I rang the buzzer on the intercom and called out, "Hello."

It spit out some static, and then a voice said, "Yes. What's your name? Do you have an appointment?"

"No, and my name is the same as yesterday and the day before that. Mark Christian. I'm a private investigator…"

"Go away. This is private property."

"I just have a couple of…"

"Fuck off. This is your last warning." It was a different voice this time, deeper and more menacing. Someone else had definitely stepped up to the intercom mike. Good. At least I had their attention.

I believe it was Goethe who said, "Act boldly, and powerful forces will come to your aid." This seemed like an appropriate time.

I walked around to the brick wall on the left. It was only six feet high, and I pulled myself up and over easily, landing on my feet on the other side. I was taking a big gamble, guessing that Tommy E. would not kill me on his property, given the fact that he was under almost constant surveillance, and that the FBI, DEA, and local police were looking for any excuse to arrest him. I was gambling that he would use non-lethal force to try to remove me.

I started to walk towards the mansion when a big guy ran out the front door, holding a large dog on a short leash. He let go of the leash and the dog charged straight for me.

It was a black rottwieler, thickly muscled with teeth bared, growling viciously and snapping its jaws as it barreled forward. Its mouth was already trailing saliva in a long lumpy string in anticipation of the coming meal, me.

I stood still, feeling myself enter that crystalline place of perfect calm that often came in moments of danger. It was meditative on the surface but charged beneath with an explosive fury. I had first felt it the night I put my uncle in the hospital, the last night he ever tried to abuse me.

The dog leapt at my throat, and I side-stepped to the right, jamming my stun gun into the side of its face. Astonishment flashed for a millisecond as I wondered how it got in my hand; I had no recollection of drawing it. 200,000 volts shot through the dog's body, disrupting the signals from its brain to its muscles. It jerked violently in mid-air, then stiffened in a grotesque position, and dropped as if dead. It lay on the lawn motionless, paralyzed, panting frantically in pain and fear. No permanent damage was done; the dog would feel fine in a few minutes.

I put the stun gun on safe—it looked kind of like an electric shaver with two prongs on the end—and slipped it back into my waist band, then started walking towards the house again.

The guy who had released the dog already had a 9mm out, pointing in my direction. I put my hands up and kept walking towards him, stopping about fifteen feet away.

He said with finality, "Now you leave."

Shit. What could I do now? Shoot him? That wouldn't accomplish anything, and he was too far away to grab the gun.

Checkmate.

I started to turn to walk away when a voice from the house said, "Hold it! Let ME see that motherfucker before he goes."

I turned back around and there was Tommy E. striding out of the house, flanked by two huge bodyguards holding shotguns. I looked him over as he approached, my hands still held high in the air. He was medium height and had a big gut. Dark skinned, shaved head, wearing designer sweats and lots of expensive, but tacky, jewelry. Your standard D.C. gangster get-up.

At first sight, he was disappointing, not at all resembling the mental image I had formed from his legend, but as he came forward, I started to reevaluate. It was his eyes. They were extraordinary; ice cold, supremely confident, and slightly glazed with insanity. I knew instantly that this was a person who inspired fear not by his size or skills, but by his utter lack of any moral limits.

He stopped an inch from my face and looked me in the eyes. To my surprise, I had an impulse to look away. It took willpower not to, because there was an almost overwhelming force about him. Without warning or hesitation, he hit me with a right hook above the left eye. I felt a ring on his hand make the contact and open up my forehead. It was a good hit and I took two steps back, but didn't go down.

"That's for hurtin' my dog, motherfucker. He better be ok, or you're a dead man. Shit, maybe you're a dead man anyway!"

"The dog will be fine in about ten minutes," I said, wiping the blood out of my left eye. It was dripping onto my shirt and the grass too. I was definitely going to need a couple of stitches. "I used a stun gun."

"Nice shot by the way," I added, referring to his punch. I was walking a very fine line and thought that the compliment might help him regain face. I had trespassed onto his property and hurt his dog, and he was feeling the disrespect. Guys like Tommy will die before they let themselves be disrespected, so I needed to pull things back now to achieve my objective.

"Tony, take his weapons," Tommy barked to one of his guys.

Tony came over quickly and frisked me, taking the .45, the stun gun, and a knife I had in my boot. I had dressed for the occasion.

"You are either the craziest white boy I ever met or the bravest. What the hell do you think you're doin'?" Tommy demanded.

"I'm looking for Carla Jones. I've been hired by her family to look for her. Rumor has it she was last seen working for you."

"You what!? That's it!? You've got to be kidding. Yo, this white boy IS crazy," Tommy said to his guys. They were spread out in a loose semi-circle on the front lawn, covering me with their weapons.

Tommy turned back to me and screamed, "Why in the fuck should I tell you anything, BITCH! What have you done for me lately besides disrespect my house.

What you SHOULD be telling me is why I shouldn't bust a cap in your ass right now!!"

Pull it back, I thought. *You got him out of his fortress to talk to you, now you got to redirect things.* "I'm sorry about that. No disrespect intended. I was just going to come up and knock on the door when the dog came after me. I used the stun gun 'cause I didn't want to do any permanent damage."

"ANSWER MY QUESTION, BITCH!" he yelled into my face. "Why in the fuck should I help you?! What can you do for ME?!"

I paused before answering, trying to think things through. I was getting nowhere so perhaps it was time to "release the four hands." It's a strategy from Musashi's *Book of Five Rings*, and it basically states that if your current approach is making no progress, don't hesitate to drop it and try a completely different one.

"All I've got to offer is entertainment," I said calmly. "I'll take on your best guy— hand-to-hand—no weapons. If I win, you tell me where Carla is. If he wins, you get to enjoy watching me get my ass beat. Either way, you get entertained; you win."

Tommy took a step back. This took him completely by surprise. "Yo, guys, what do you think? Our own Friday night fights!"

"Sounds all right, Tommy," the guy who frisked me said. "I say we put him up against Big Maurice. Won't be much of a fight, though. This guy won't last one minute with him."

"Shiit, white boy! You're on. Just when I thought I'd seen everything there is to see! Come on in to my gym, and we'll get started."

I went into the house at the point of a gun. The house was just as I suspected; tacky, showy rich. Black velvet drapes, a rug with a huge TE monogrammed on it, a home movie theatre, and a six-foot-long fish tank. Gold embroidered furniture.

They took me into Tommy's home gym. It was about as big as my whole house, lined with an assortment of exercise machines. Surprisingly, there were no mirrors. Then again, maybe it wasn't so surprising. If I had done the things that Tommy had, I wouldn't want to look at myself in the mirror, either.

I was led onto a large exercise mat in the center of the room and frisked again. This time they were checking to see if I was wired. They checked my PI's license. I could hear someone calling for Maurice, my opponent. A couple of more guys filed in, and everyone passed around some beers and a spliff. They sat on the exercise machines or stood against the wall. Tommy E. sat on the only chair in the room, talking to an associate, a huge grin on his face. They were all chattering excitedly and predicting my swift destruction. More than a few times they pointed at me and laughed.

I took off my black leather coat. The laughing died down.

"Yo, man! Where'd you get cut up like that? You just get out of prison?" one of them called out to me.

Among criminals, when someone is built, it's usually because they've just done some time. There isn't much to do in prison but work out, and a lot of guys do it to pass the time and get an intimidating build, hoping that it will deter attacks.

"Sort of. The Marine Corps."

"Well, the guy you goin' to fight used to be a linebacker with the Redskins."

"Really. What's his name?"

"Maurice Jackson," one of them yelled out.

I smiled. "Never heard of him. What was he, fifth string?"

"Fourth string!" Tommy E. yelled out. Everyone cracked up. Got to laugh when the boss makes a joke. I didn't bother.

Maurice walked in.

A cheer went up, and his friends called out his name and yelled things like, "We got a white boy for you to whip! Don't kill him too fast Maurice!"

He was a mountain of a man. About 6'6" and 350 pounds, with arms the size of my waist and shoulders twice as broad as mine. He was thick around the middle, and his muscle tone was poor, he had obviously let himself go since his days as an athlete. Nevertheless, he looked awesome.

He came forward and stopped about four feet away from me, looking down at me from his great height with calm, absolute confidence. I wasn't surprised; a guy the size of Maurice had undoubtedly been intimidating people his whole life, and he naturally had an unshakeable belief that this would not be different. That was good. It meant that he would underestimate me. Because large guys like him could intimidate most people so easily, they rarely developed any exceptional street-fighting skills.

I had learned hand-to-hand fighting in the Special Forces, using British Special Air Service (SAS) techniques.

There was no harm in encouraging his overconfidence, so I turned to a guy in the corner and said, "Can you throw me that towel, my head really hurts."

A chorus of jeers went up. "Oh, poor baby, just wait till Maurice hits your ass," and so on and so forth.

The guy in the corner threw me the towel, and I made a great show of dabbing the cut above my eye, grimacing in pain. Maurice was laughing now, totally at ease.

"Ok, boys, lets get it on!!" yelled Tommy E.

A cheer went up, and Maurice just stood there laughing.

I had been bent over, dabbing my cut. Now I dropped the towel and stood straight up and looked Maurice in the eyes. I could tell that he was surprised at my transformation, and a shadow of doubt crossed his face for the first time.

I needed to make him commit, to come at me. I said in a loud, condescending voice, "Hey Maurice! Is it true that all you football players are gay? Always slapping each other on the ass. Bending over to hike the ball and shit? Do you like a nice fat dick up your ass, Maurice?"

"Oh, shit," he said smiling. "Now I'm going to have to hurt you."

He shot his huge arm out to grab me, and I trapped it, then grabbed his pinkie with one hand, and snapped it back violently. If Maurice had gone with the direction I was twisting, he would have been fine, albeit on his back. But he stood fast, and it snapped.

He tore the finger out of my hand, yelling out in pain. He backed away and looked at his pinkie, gaping in disbelief; it hung limply to the side at an sickening, unnatural angle.

Pain then gave way to anger, and he rushed back at me, swinging the other arm. It was a good fast swing for a man his size, and it caught me on the top of my head as I ducked down and planted my motorcycle boot right between his legs.

To say that Maurice hit me is the wrong word. The Biblical term "smite" is more accurate. His fist only glanced off the top of my head, but it snapped my neck to the side, and I collapsed as I was giving him my boot. My head was ringing, and I knew that if he had caught me with a square shot, it might have killed me. At the very least, it would have put me out. As soon as I could, I stood up.

Maurice was still down. He had vomited on the floor and was holding his crotch with his good hand and screaming in agony.

The room was deathly silent.

Tommy E. got up and walked over to Maurice. "Get up you fucking, no good pussy! Get your ass up!"

Through force of will and fury, Maurice got slowly to his feet, then staggered over to me and took another swing with his good hand, the other still covering his crotch, his face twisted in pain. This time the swing was slower and I dodged it easily and hit him as hard as I could, aiming at his neck just to the left of the windpipe. I didn't want to hit it straight on, or it might have collapsed it and killed him. He made a strange "Kacck" sound as my fist connected and fell flat on his back, struggling now to breathe through his bruised windpipe.

It was over.

The room was deathly silent until someone exclaimed, "shiiiit!"

Someone else said, "Goddamn! He beat big Maurice! Ain't no one ever done that before."

I looked over at Tommy E. He was looking down at Maurice with disdain.

"So Tommy," I said, holding my head. It was killing me. "We made a deal. I win; you tell me where Carla is." It was a statement that was really a question. Would he keep his end of the bargain?

"Fuck you! Find her yourself! Tony, get him outa here," Tommy barked viciously to one of his men. He turned back to me and said, "If me or one of my boys ever see you again, you're dead."

Tony escorted me out of the house at gunpoint, and down the driveway to the gate. When we got there he pushed a button and the gate slowly swung open. I stood there despondent, dizzy with pain, more than willing to pick up where Maurice had left off and beat myself up. *Of all the stupid, impulsive, dumb, useless plans. All this for nothing.* Then I shrugged to myself and thought, *If you make a deal with the devil, don't be surprised if he reneges.*

Tony returned my weapons and then stepped back, looking at me strangely, as if he was trying to come to a decision. Finally he took a deep breath and said, "You did all right in there, and there ain't no harm in you knowing where Carla is. Tommy's just mad 'cause you made one of his best boys look like a chump. Carla got AIDS from shooting up with dirty needles. Last I heard she was in D.C. General. She's probably dead by now."

"Tony, thanks. Really." I was flooded with relief.

"Yeah, well, if you want to thank me, do it by keeping your mouth shut about who told you."

I nodded and walked out.

-12-

Back in the city, swimming in the sidewalk currents. A river of faces flow past, fading into forever. Here before me and then gone to their fate. Wrapped within themselves, they look into the middle distance, hiding in plain sight. Within a mile I have passed maybe a thousand people, a random sample of humanity that likely includes at least one murderer and one saint. They are wrapped in packages that conceal the humanity beneath; corporate package, parent package, power package, neo-hippie, pseudo saint.

Up a winding stairwell, carved wood and fading paint. At the top floor I go down the hallway and stop at a door, then gently knock. Aislinn opens the door, her face projecting joy that quickly turns to shock.

"What happened to you?!"

"It's nothing. A work-related injury. I got a couple of stitches." I then proceeded to give her a sanitized version of the day's events. No sense in freaking her out completely.

"Oh my God, come in. Sit down," she exclaimed after I finished.

"No, that's alright. I just wanted to see you."

Aislinn pushed me down into a chair and ran her slender hand gently around the bandage on my forehead, as if to verify it's reality by touch. Then she looked higher and said, "You've got a big lump on your head, too!"

"Yeah, and a mild concussion, according to the doctor."

"Oh honey!" she said, kissing me softly on the lips.

I could tell that she was going into full caretaker mode, and I was looking forward to surrendering to it completely. Nothing like a little nurturing after a day like today. When you're around people with dirty, diseased souls, a little love from a good person is like an emotional cleansing. It restores your faith in humanity and reminds you of what you are, in the broadest sense, striving to protect: the possibility of good in the world, of safety and security for decent people. I also desperately wanted to make love. My sex drive usually skyrocketed right after any proximity to danger.

As she fussed over me, I said, "You're so beautiful. I could look at you forever." It wasn't a line. At that moment, I felt it absolutely.

She smiled, delighted, and leaned over to kiss me. The kisses became more passionate, and without conscious thought we were on the floor, tearing off clothes. We made quick, intense, spectacular love and then lay exhausted on the thick rug, holding each other closely and reverently, exchanging slow, deep kisses as we came down from heaven. We lay there a long time, loving the feel of our bodies together.

Later she said jokingly, "That was wonderful. You should get beat up more often."

"Hey, I didn't get beat up."

"Danger, male-ego alert. Compliment immediately," she said in a faux-computer voice. Then using an exaggerated, seductive female voice, she said, "Oh, baby, you're such a tough, manly man."

Her delivery was great, and I broke up laughing. It made my head explode in pain. I reached over and grabbed my jeans and pulled out a bottle of Tylenol with codeine. *Thank you, doctor,* I thought as I walked naked into the kitchen to get some water.

On my way back, Aislinn said, "New rule in my apartment. I'm not giving you your clothes back. You must be naked at all times." She was lying on the floor watching me, smiling wickedly, still naked herself, looking gorgeous.

"Only if you lead by example," I replied.

Aislinn saw me grimace in pain as I lay back down, and it put her back into full caretaker mode. She put me in her bed, insisting that I rest for the remainder of the day. She made some hot tea, then went out and bought me some magazines to read.

However embarrassing it is to admit, this ex-marine, combat veteran, sometime tough guy, loved every minute of it. I made a mental note to return the favor someday soon. Within an hour, the pain pills had fully kicked in, and I drifted off to sleep.

I awoke the next morning to the sounds of Aislinn cooking in the kitchenette with various loud clatters, bangs, and scrapes. *Damn*, I thought grumpily, *is she cooking or doing minor construction*? I rolled over and pulled a pillow over my head, desperate for some more sleep. I tried to drift off again, until the smell of coffee convinced me to blearily open my eyes and call out, "Caffeine!"

Head still under the pillow, I fumbled around for the pack of cigarettes I had left on the windowsill. Just as I grabbed them, the pillow lifted off my head, and a mug of coffee swam into view.

"Bless you and all the generations of your family," I said groggily.

Aislinn chuckled and then went back to cooking. I climbed out onto the fire escape to have the coffee and a cigarette. By the time I came back in, I was in a better mood. I sat down at her table with my back to the wall so I could see the city view.

"I thought you didn't cook," I called out to her.

"I can when I want to. I just don't want to very often," she called back.

A while later, she came out of the kitchenette carrying two plates stacked high with scrambled eggs, sausage, toast, and home fries.

"Perfect early-morning food," I said appreciatively.

"Thanks. I figured you'd be revolted by anything remotely healthy."

"Ah...further proof that the curative powers of cholesterol are overlooked and underappreciated."

"And what exactly are the curative powers of cholesterol?" she asked.

"Well, I have a theory that the fat in the cholesterol absorbs the large quantities of caffeine that I drink, leaving just enough to, in turn, counteract the calming effects of the nicotine, thereby leaving me....normal."

She laughed. "Do you work so hard at all your rationalizations?"

"Who doesn't?"

"Good point."

I turned my full attention to the food, sneaking occasional glances at Aislinn as she ate and read the Federal Page of the Post. She was wearing my shirt from yesterday, which she had washed clean of blood stains. Her beautiful legs and feet were bare and elegantly crossed.

At one point when she lowered the paper to take a bite of toast, I said, "Being a trained investigator, I see that we've graduated to the 'wearing each other's clothes' phase of a relationship."

Aislinn smiled. "As long as I don't catch you wearing my heels. Then we're definitely back to square one."

After breakfast I did the dishes, and Aislinn disappeared into the bathroom to do whatever it is that women do in there for hours at a time.

When she finished, she said, "I have a surprise for you. Follow me."

She took my hand and led me out of the apartment. We walked to the end of her musty, poorly lit hallway and then up a stairway that led to the roof. The door at the top was unlocked, and when we walked out onto the flat roof, we were hit with a spectacular view of the city.

"It's incredible, isn't it?" Aislinn said. "Look, you can see all the way down to the monuments."

"I love it," I said. "You must be on the highest hill in the city."

We made two trips back to the apartment to get lawn chairs, drinks, and something to read. After we got settled, I spent some time gazing at the immensity of the sky. A cluster of gray bottom clouds rode the warm wind eastwards, and a few birds floated in circles above us, angels in blue.

"You love it so much," Aislinn said, looking at me kindly. "You always seem so content in high places. Why is that?"

"At the risk of sounding like an amateur shrink, it goes back to childhood."

"Childhood? How so?" she asked.

I looked at her expression and decided that it was not a casual or rhetorical question. She seemed genuinely interested in knowing more about me.

"Well, it will take a while to explain but I'll try. As you know my parents died in a car accident when I was young, and I went to live with my only living relative, my uncle. I hadn't known him well before then. I realized later that my parents had made it a point not to visit often. All I can remember is just being grateful that I had somewhere to go. I had fantasies of my uncle's family being loving and replacing what I had lost when my parents died. It didn't turn out that way. Not even close."

"My uncle was tolerable when sober, but when he drank—which was nearly every night—he became vicious. He beat my aunt and cousins over the slightest annoyance, and he got annoyed a lot. He couldn't handle the responsibility of a family, and he quickly came to resent me for adding to what he thought was an intolerable burden. I became the most frequent target. I was small as a kid and terrified, and no one came to my defense. My aunt and cousins were so relieved that most of the abuse was directed at me, they couldn't bring themselves to try to stop it. Most days I went to school I had at least a couple of bruises under my clothes; he was always careful never to hit me in the face. And his mouth! God, that fucker said the most horrible things to me. Sometimes that was worse than the beatings."

I stopped to take a deep breath, trying to stifle the rage that rose within me whenever I talked about this.

"At first I tried appeasement. Maybe if I became hypervigilant to my uncle's every need, he would stop hitting me. I nearly killed myself trying to keep him happy, and it worked to reduce his rage a little bit, but it didn't come close to stopping it."

"Then I tried escape. I remember the first day that I decided not to come home after school. I walked into the woods and climbed this mountain that looked down on the town we lived in. As I neared the top, I started to feel safe and serene for the first time in a very long time. I mean the feeling hit me like a shot of morphine. It was total bliss."

"Why did you feel so safe up there?" Aislinn asked.

"I think it was because the mountain was very steep and uninhabited, and I knew that no one could find me there. So there was no possibility of being hit or screamed at. Anyway, ever since then, I've had a very strong attraction to high places."

"What happened when you came down off the mountain?" she asked.

"It was very bad. I didn't come home all that night and didn't go to school the next day. I just slept up there and idled the whole next day away. I couldn't bring myself to come down. When I finally did, I got the worst beating ever. He knocked a back tooth out, blackened both my eyes, and ripped my back open whipping me with an electric cord. Then he made me clean up my own blood, which was all over the floor. That night I cried and cried for hours feeling totally hopeless, and then he came into my room and beat me again for crying too much."

"At that moment it hit me like a bullet between the eyes—*the answer*. It was absolutely clear. I had to become stronger than my uncle in every way so that I could beat him. I had to take away his means of controlling me and making me afraid. I had to build myself up to the point where I could dominate him physically and psychologically. That was the only way the abuse would stop."

"I began to work out obsessively and read countless books on self-defense. I would pick out particular techniques and practice them thousands of times a day. I stole a pair of boxing gloves from a sporting goods store and would go out into the woods and pound on the trees until my hands felt broken. By my sixteenth birthday, I was ready.

"That night my uncle came home more drunk that usual and started to lay into me. This red rage exploded from within me. Four years of anger came out in four minutes. I have very little conscious memory of what happened, just a few flashbulb-like memories. All I know is when I finally started to calm down enough to see straight, my uncle was on the kitchen floor, unconscious and nearly dead. I broke his jaw, two of his ribs, and his right arm. I split his skull open with a pan. I had knocked all his front teeth out. My uncle ended up staying in intensive care for two weeks. He nearly died from internal bleeding. My aunt called the police and I was locked up in a juvenile detention center."

I paused and looked at Aislinn. She looked both sad and horrified.

"When my sentencing hearing came up, the judge took me into his chambers and asked me why I had attacked my uncle. I told him everything about what I had been through and, thank God, he had enough sense to believe me. He reduced my sentence to time served and had me wait in chambers until his day was done. He drove me to his church and talked to the Priest there. Then they both asked me if I wanted to go live in a Catholic seminary. Given the alternative, I said *yes*."

There was silence for a time. Eventually Aislinn reached over to hold my hand and said, "Thanks."

"Thanks for what?"

"For letting me in a little bit."

-13-

I was standing in a brightly lit hallway in D.C. General Hospital, trying to get some information about Carla Jones's condition from a harried nurse.

"She has systemic candidiasis, MAI, and is in the final stages of a pneumosystis infection. At our last test she had twenty-nine T cells left."

"I have no idea what you just said," I replied.

"She's going to die within a week or two," the nurse said flatly. "Look, I've got other patients waiting on me. If you want to see her, she's in Room 601." With that she turned and walked away.

"Thanks," I said to her back.

Carla lay in her bed, little more than a wraith beneath the covers. She couldn't have weighed more than seventy-five pounds, eyes bulging in her sunken face. Her skin was an unnatural greyish pallor, like she was dead already.

Before I could introduce myself, she broke into a fit of coughing so severe that it sounded as her lungs would come up. Spittle sprayed across the room, and I took a step backwards to avoid it.

When she finished, she looked me over and said bitterly, "It figures my last visitor would be a cop."

"I'm not a cop. I'm a private investigator."

"What do you want?" she said with a sigh. It was clear she didn't give a fuck what I wanted. Understandable, given her condition.

"I'm trying to find out who killed your cousin Eric."

"So?"

"Do you know what happened to him?" I asked a little more sharply than I had intended.

"I heard on the street that someone smoked him. So what? He never did nothin' for me."

"Someone hit him twice in the stomach with a shotgun. Nearly blew him in half. I thought you might be bothered by that."

"Fuck him!! Now go away!"

I could feel my anger quickly rising and fought hard to keep it in check. Clearly, this was not someone who had experienced any deathbed epiphanies. I felt powerless, not knowing what else to say or do.

I walked out and went down to the first-floor lobby to think. It wasn't too long before I had an idea. I went to the pay phone and called Greg.

"Hey buddy!" he exclaimed. "I had a great time out at your place, despite the bear."

"Me too. Listen, Greg, I need your help." I explained the situation, and he said that he'd be over right away.

He arrived an hour later, dressed in full-priest regalia. Every time I saw him like that, it always took me a minute to adjust. This was not my easygoing buddy Greg, who used to pick his nose in class when we were teens. It was not even the guy who had just hung out at my house for a couple of days. This was *Father* Greg Bearant of the Holy Roman Catholic Church. The effect was made all the more powerful by the pure compassion and dignity that he genuinely projected.

We went upstairs, and Greg went into Carla's room.

I leaned against the wall in the hallway, out of sight. For a long time I could hear Greg's soft voice murmuring and Carla's strident one in response. I couldn't hear what they were saying, but I had absolute faith that Greg knew what he was doing, so I stopped trying to listen and tuned out.

Nurses and visitors passed intermittently in the hallway. Occasionally, I caught a whiff of that hospital smell I hated. It was a mix of chemicals and sickness and decay.

One very large nurse looked me up and down every time she went by on errands, and then settled into the nurses' station to do her charting. Eventually she tried to sneak another look at me, and I smiled back at her in response. I had no intentions, she just seemed nice, and I appreciated the compliment. She looked a bit embarrassed at being caught looking and quickly went back to her work.

I shifted positions; it had been almost two hours, and my legs were starting to feel numb. *Maybe I'll get a seat in the waiting room.*

There was crying coming out of Carla's room now. Greg, the Barbara Walters of the priesthood. He was legendary for his ability to make people cry in a good way, as a release of their deepest pain. We used to kid him about it in the seminary. We would wait until he said something innocuous like *good morning* or *pass the ketchup,* and we would break into mock tears. I smiled at the memory and tried to figure out how he did it. Perhaps it was the unconditional acceptance he gave to everyone. You never got a sense that he was judging you... and so eventually could let your guard down, and let it all come out.

Greg came out of her room and said, "She wants us to call her family and ask them to visit."

"I'll do it right now."

It took awhile as I had to track down both Lillian and Pat at work. When they arrived, I met them downstairs in the hospital lobby.

Lillian embraced me and said jokingly, "Well at least your accomplishin' somethin' with my money!"

I laughed, and the two women thanked me profusely. I told them I had found Carla, but my friend Greg deserved the real credit. He had inspired her to seek a reconciliation with her family.

"Have you found out who killed my boy yet?" Lillian asked.

"No, I'm sorry. I'm not even close, but I'm still working on it."

With that, the two ladies said goodbye and left for Carla's room. I watched them walk away. They carried themselves with a hard won dignity, and quiet strength.

An hour later Greg came down. He sank into a chair and said, "I left them to be alone with each other. I think it went well." Greg's head sunk down onto the back of his chair, and his eyes were blank. He was completely drained. I'd seen it before. His work was so emotionally intense that it often wasted him. He would need some time alone to recoup and be ready for the next spiritual crisis.

"You did some good today, buddy. Thanks," I said. "Did she know anything about Eric's murder?"

"No. She said that in her years on the street, she only heard one thing that related to Eric. That a guy working at the Government Printing Office was in the life and connected to some big people on the street. It stuck in her mind not because she thought it had anything to do with the murder, but because she knew that Eric worked there. She said his name is Fredericks. Mean anything?"

"No. But I'll follow up on it."

When I pulled into Trinity Holy Redeemer Church in Manassas, all that remained of the day was a red sliver on the horizon. I had arranged another meeting here with Eric's old boss, Phillip Riley. I had called him from D.C. General, informed him that I was still investigating Eric's murder, and wanted to question him further about one of his employees. He said that he was busy, but if it was urgent, he could meet me at his church after work. He was volunteering there until the late evening.

As I strode into the church, old ladies scattered like seagulls on a sidewalk. I tried not to be hurt. With my leathers, motorcycle boots, and .45 showing in a side holster, I probably looked like I was there to rob the place. I gave them my best *I'm a nice guy* reassuring smile, and they only drew back farther. Their eyes widened, and they glanced at each other, as if my smile had only confirmed their suspicions.

"Does anyone here know Phillip Riley?" I asked into the awkward space.

"Are you a friend of his?" one of the old ladies asked tentatively, afraid I'd say yes.

"Not exactly," I said. "I'm here to ask him for his daughter's hand in marriage."

"Oh, how wonderful," another lady said, but her eyes said something else.

"Thanks. You're all welcome to the reception. It's going to be held at a rock concert. The lead singer is going to lead us through our vows. Then we're going to a nudist colony for our honeymoon."

They finally got it and tittered politely.

"Actually, I'm a private investigator." I held up my license, and they relaxed a bit. "Where is Mr. Riley?"

"He's in the basement meeting hall. He volunteers in the kitchen down there every Wednesday night. We have a walk-in dinner for the local homeless people."

"Thanks," I said, still smiling.

I found him hunched over a huge pot, scrubbing away. Apparently I had missed the dinner and had entered during the cleanup phase. Phil looked up and waved, saying, "I'll be with you as soon as I'm done with this."

"Ok."

I sat down and looked around. Most of the volunteers were older, with a couple of middle-aged exceptions. Their eyes had the full, peaceful look of the faithful in service to something good. They swirled around, completely engaged in the cleanup, but it already felt clean here, spiritually speaking.

Only one person looked anxious. He was intensely lecturing another volunteer on the proper way to stack the chairs in a corner. He seemed like one of those people who had spent his whole life consumed by petty urgencies. Then again, he could just be having a bad day.

Phil Riley plopped down in the seat opposite me and pushed a slice of cake across the table. "Leftovers," he said. "Have some."

"Thanks. Nice thing you do here." I said.

"Yes. It helps a lot of local families. Where do you worship?" He asked the question with thinly veiled condescension, having already guessed that I did not go to church.

"Everywhere. I'm never not in church."

He looked confused but didn't try to clarify.

"So why did you want to see me again? Have you found out who killed Eric?" he asked eagerly.

"No," I said. "But I'd like to interview one of your employees whose name came up during the investigation. It's probably nothing but I'd like to check into it. His name is Fredericks."

"Jack Fredericks. Sure. He's a long-time employee. Eric was his direct supervisor."

"What are your impressions of him?"

"He's a harmless loser. About four years ago, he came up positive on a drug test, and we sent him to our EAP program. He's come up clean ever since. A mediocre employee but definitely doesn't strike me as a killer."

"Mind if I talk to him?"

"Of course not. But I'd prefer if you didn't do it at work. It would cause a lot of crazy rumors and questions. I'll slip you his home address, off the record, of course. Legally I can't ever release an employees address to a third party."

"Thanks. You've been a great help, and I appreciate it."

I left Manassas and went to my office in Old Town Warrenton, in the foothills of the mountains. I sank into my desk chair, fished out a lighter and some cigarettes, then sat a while, smoking and staring blankly at the walls. Good to keep busy. Eventually, I picked up the stereo remote and on came Coltrane's "Softly as a Morning Sunrise." Artie Shaw was on piano, his notes skipping and dancing like an irregular rain. Coltrane came in right behind, riding on top of everything with a lazy mastery. It was Shaw I stayed focused on though, because I loved the way he'd mastered that uniquely jazz art of making his fingers sound as if they've tripped into place on the keys. As if he didn't quite know what he was going to play next, and each note was a revelation.

It was a great piece, but a little out of synch with my mood. The next cut, "Soul Eyes," was better, with Coltrane's sax blowing riffs that were sparse and dismal and filled with yearning. It got me to thinking about Aislinn and our couple of days together.

I lit a second cigarette and looked around at my office. It was a bit ratty, to put it kindly. A sagging couch, scarred desk, and swivel chair. Between the two windows was my stereo, the glow of the equalizer rising and falling in rhythm with the music in a waterfall of red and green lights. It was a pleasing, festive counterpoint to the darkness of the room.

The phone rang, and I picked up. It was Butch De Carlo.

"I've been trying to reach you for the last two days!" he said.

"I was in the city, staying with Aislinn. What's up?"

"You've become a legend here at DEA."

"Huh?" I said, waiting for the punch line.

"We've had Tommy E.'s house wired for over two months. When you fought his guy, we heard the whole thing. The guys in the monitoring van brought the tape back, and we played it in staff meeting. You should have heard the cheering, buddy. Way to go!"

"Butch, is this one of your sick jokes?"

"I swear I've told the whole truth and nothing but the truth."

"Damn."

"Well, listen, we were so psyched that a couple of us volunteered to put some office time into finding that woman for you."

"Oh thanks, but I already found her. She's in D.C. General."

"Well, if there is anything we can ever do, let us know," Butch said. "You have no idea how much we enjoyed that whole thing. We're so locked up in rules and buearacracy that it was joyous—fucking joyous— to see someone just walk in and beat the shit out of Tommy's best boy and make him look like a mark."

"Thanks, buddy. I may take you up on that someday. He threatened my life, but it struck me as a passive threat. If it ever becomes an active one I may need some backup."

"You got it."

-14-

The next morning I was standing in front of a row house in Northwest Washington D.C. On the corner, about 15 yards away, stood a group of young men. They all had blue bandanas wrapped tightly around their heads, and were whiling away the day, smoking Newports and talking. On the other side of the street, a woman walked a little dog, the kind that a friend of mine derisively called "yappers."

I knocked on the door of the row house. The door cracked open slightly, and one eye peeked out from behind it.

"Who the fuck are you?"

"Are you Jack Fredericks?" I asked.

"Yeah." The voice was tentative, suspicious.

"My name is Mark Christian. I'm a private detective hired by Lillian Jones. I wanted to talk to you about the murder of her son Eric."

"I don't know..."

"Listen," I said casually. "This is no big deal. I'm interviewing a lot of people who knew him or worked with him."

There was a pause. "Alright, but you can't stay long. Got some people comin' over later."

I took a long look at Fredericks as he let me in. White, around thirty years old and twenty pounds underweight. I doubted that it was due to aerobics.

The house was a catastrophe, far beyond the stereotypical bachelor mess. It was the kind of place where you wipe your feet when you leave. At his invitation, I threw a pile of crap off the sofa and sat down.

"So," I said. "I understand that Eric was your supervisor."

"Yes."

"How long did you work for him?"

"Six years."

He was avoiding eye contact, absently picking at his big toe. It was an ugly toe, turned green with fungus.

"You know they have medicine for that nowadays," I said, gesturing vaguely in the direction of his bare foot.

He looked at me blankly.

"It's amazing the advances in medical science."

Still, he ignored me.

"Are you on drugs?" I asked him sharply.

That got his attention. His eyes widened, and he paused before answering, trying to decide what to say.

"I used to be. I stopped about three years ago."

"What did you do?"

"Heroin and crack."

"Did you know that Eric was killed in a drive-by and that it was drug related?

"Yeah. They were saying around work it was a case of mistaken identity. That the guys who did it thought Eric was someone else."

"That's the police line, but I doubt it," I said. "I find it more interesting that one of his employees has a history of drug use."

"Hey! I had nothin' to do with it. I was workin' overtime the night he was killed."

"I know, your boss—Mr. Riley—called this morning to tell me."

"Then why are you hassling me?"

"You were in the life," I said. "Maybe you've heard something that I haven't. Maybe you know who did it."

"I don't, really. Wish I did, but I don't. Eric was all right, and I wasn't happy to see him killed," he said. "Listen, I got somewhere to go, so you need to get out of here now."

"I thought you said you had people coming over."

"Whatever. Get the fuck out."

"Fine. But understand this. If I find out you knew something about Eric's murder and didn't tell me, I'll make it my personal mission in life to make you miserable."

Outside, as I got on my Triumph and prepared to leave, I thought about Fredericks. The interview didn't sit right. My gut was telling me that he was still into drugs and knew more about Eric Jones' murder than he was letting on. Another part of me, however, was skeptical of these feelings. I knew that I was desperate for a lead and could be making something out of nothing. I decided to look into things further.

The next day I went back to shake down Fredericks' place while he was at work. I jimmied the door open easily and I closed it carefully behind me as I entered the musty foyer, listening intently for the sounds of someone else in the house. An empty coat rack, stairwell leading upwards, and naked hardwood floors, cracked and fading. A rustling nearby, and I stopped, reaching for my gun until I caught myself, realizing that it was probably some rodent.

After a minute of so of silence, I was reassured sufficiently to start up the stairs. They creaked loudly with each step, and I winced inwardly at the noise.

At the top was a small hallway leading into the main bedroom. There was a bathroom and bedroom off to the sides. I went into the bathroom, and the walls were covered in blood. There was dried vomit around the toilet rim and on the floor.

I stopped a moment, stunned, before leaning forward to take a closer look. The blood on the walls had long since dried, having come off in places in coppery flakes that lay on the tile floor. It clung to the wall in small, nebular splatters that I couldn't make sense of. If someone had been shot or stabbed in here, the pattern would be different.

Then I turned and saw the dirty syringe in the washbasin and figured it out. Fredericks would have to clear the syringe after each time he shot up heroin, splattering blood on the walls in just the way I was seeing. That would account for the vomit, too. I remember my friend James, a substance abuse counselor, telling me once that the body reacts to heroin as it would poison, making a person throw up almost immediately after injection.

I left the bathroom and went into the master bedroom. The morning light came in narrow shafts through the slats of the partially drawn shades, lifting the darkness of the room a little. There was a bare mattress, marred by stains and cigarette burns, and clothes and filthy dishes and glasses strewn about the floor. An overturned ashtray lay next to the bed, with ashes and cigarette butts landing in a wide circle on the rug.

J.D. Miller

I took a couple of steps into the room and heard the sharp sound of glass breaking. I lifted my boot, and the front half of a syringe came up with it, the needle sticking out of the sole of my shoe. A small wave of revulsion and fear ran through me. I grabbed a shirt off the floor and wrapped it around my hand, using it for protection as I pulled out the syringe. Then, with a feeling of dreadful urgency, I sat on the bed and took off the boot and checked my foot. No puncture wound. Hell, it hadn't even gone all the way through the bottom of the boot.

I said a small prayer of thanks, flooded with relief. I remembered Sterling telling me that the majority of heroin addicts in the city had HIV. A centimeter of rubber had possibly averted my slow death.

I tossed the room for the next hour with exaggerated care, pausing to look before every step, careful to put things back where I had found them.

In the top drawer of the nightstand I found three more syringes, a spoon that was burned brown on the bottom, a foot length of thin rubber hose, a box of cotton balls, and a number of bags filled with a pure-white, powdery substance. It was high grade heroin, maybe China white, the kind of heroin that nobody could afford on a government salary. I was looking at maybe ten-grand worth right there in the drawer.

How long would it take him to go through this? Not long, if the number of blood stains on the bathroom wall was any indication. Where was he getting that kind of money?

I checked the rest of the house, looking mainly for telephone receipts. If you were going to find a lead, I knew you often found it there. Credit card receipts were good too, but I doubted that Fredericks had one. The best I could manage was an overdue electric bill. I picked up the phone and then knew why. It was dead.

Going to a streaked window in the front of the house, I scanned the street. It was empty, so I walked out of the house, got on my bike, and left.

J.D. Miller

- 15 -

The New Orleans Café was on the Adams Morgan restaurant strip, a couple of blocks down from Aislinn's apartment. It was long and narrow with mirrored walls, revolving fans, and close-set tables that were a rich clay red. We sat in front of the bay windows in the late afternoon light, having beignets and coffee.

"I'm starting to wonder if you're not suicidal or something," Aislinn said as kindly as she could manage.

"What?"

"Look at your life. The motorcycle, the cigarettes, the violence. Just three days ago, you got a concussion and stitches in your head, and now today you step on a bloody needle. What kind of person lives like that?" she exclaimed.

I had just finished telling Aislinn about my day and was now regretting it. I made a mental note to be careful what I talked about in the future. "Listen Aislinn, I'm on a bad streak. I've had years go by where nothing dangerous happens." What I didn't say was that I was excruciatingly bored those years.

"You say that, but it's not what I've seen."

"So what's your point?" I asked, even though I already knew.

"My point is that you don't seem to value your life very much—unlike the rest of the world. I don't know were it comes from. Maybe your parents dying when you were young and your horrible experience with your uncle made you believe that life was such a perilous, ephemeral place that it wasn't worth worrying about survival. Or maybe you're hooked on the adrenaline. I don't know. I just don't think it's sane or normal."

"Who wants to be normal?"

"I do, some of our friends do, most of humanity does," she responded.

"So what would you have me do? Get an accounting degree and a nine-to-five job, enslave myself to a big mortgage, and spend the rest of my life yelling at the kids and mowing the lawn?"

"What's wrong with that?" Aislinn said with a forced calm. We respected each other so we were both making an effort to keep things cool, but I could feel the anger growing with each exchange.

"Nothing, I guess, if that's what feeds your soul. It would never work for me, though."

"Why not? Is it so impossible to think of another way of life?" she asked, exasperated.

"Yes...for me it is. Why is it so important to you that I do?"

She paused and took a deep breath. "Because I've fallen for you. Because sometimes I wish we could be together forever and make babies and do all those normal things that you despise."

I sat back stunned. A slow wave of elation rose within and I said, "I've fallen for you, too. Do you know that when you sleep sometimes I just lie there and look at you?"

"You do? Really? That's kind of creepy," she said, but she was smiling, and I could tell she was deeply flattered. She reached out and put her hand in mine. The waiter came, breaking the moment. We paused our conversation until he had poured our refills and retreated.

"But I'm scared to give my heart to you," Aislinn said. "I hold back because in these wonderful fantasies, I also see you gone for days or weeks. I see myself living constantly in fear, not sure whether you will come home at all. I see our kids growing up without a father or emulating him and becoming daredevils. And then I have to worry constantly about them, too."

"I can't argue with any of that. Guys like me make great boyfriends, but not so great husbands. But if I tried to change myself for you, I wouldn't be able to look myself in the mirror. This is what I am and what I want to be. I'm not saying that my choices are any better than anybody else's, but they are right for me, and my principles, and my personality. A basic principle that I believe in is that every person must first find their own best self, their mission in life, and then be true to it. If I tried to become something I'm not, it would be a betrayal of everything I believe in."

"Ok," Aislinn said, her face settling into lines of resignation, and I hoped eventually acceptance.

The sky quickly darkened, and there was the echo of distant thunder. The wind began to gust, and a paper cup rolled and skipped down the sidewalk as if celebrating the coming storm. The lightning came closer, the crash of each strike making the window panes near us slightly, beautifully shiver. We looked out and up just as an immense black cloud slid slowly into place over the city, like some gargantuan mother ship come to conquer the earth.

"Here comes the rain," Aislinn said, smiling.

The torrent began, and we went outside into it, holding hands and faces up to greet the downpour—as if in supplication to some ancient god. We walked, happily getting soaked through while people jogged past, holding newspapers or jackets over their bowed heads, dancing forward in odd hopscotch-like patterns to avoid the puddles.

The rain was a symphony of water, splashing it's eternal rhythm, singing an aria of joy and renewal. Aislinn laughed and kicked water at me. Her copper hair was plastered down around her head and in one exquisite, female movement, she flipped it back out of her face. I slid into her arms and kissed her until we both gasped for breath, the rain bouncing off of our noses and foreheads and shoulders.

She was soaked completely through now and began to shiver; so I took off my jacket and put it around her. We ran up the stairs, laughing and playing, and into her apartment where we began to frantically strip off clothes, throwing them carelessly aside as we made our way to the bedroom. She opened up her window so we could hear the rain, and feel the cool breeze that had delivered it. Despite the breeze, we were both soon hot and sweating and crying out our release.

Georgetown. The home of the elite of the political and media class. I watched it slide by through the streaked windows of the cab, Aislinn next to me, smiling happily in anticipation, pointing out the sights.

"Look, Mark. There's the townhouse where Jackie and JFK lived when they first came to Washington!"

"Wow," I said, not really giving a shit, but playing along as she was clearly enjoying the role of tour guide.

"There's Senator Lieberman's synagogue."

"Wow."

We were on our way to dinner at the Secretary of Commerce's home. He was a former congressman from Ohio and close friend of the President's. He was also Aislinn's boss and mentor. She usually didn't bring me to these things, because she knew they bored me to death, but wanted me to come tonight to send a clear signal to a guy named Brad, who had been pursuing her relentlessly and had even gone so far as to tell her that she would be his future wife. I also sensed that this was a test of some sort, to see if I could fit in with the type of people with whom she intended to spend her life. She had already expressed doubts about my suitability as a life-long partner, and it was a clear, unspoken expectation that tonight was my opportunity to prove her wrong.

As we pulled up in front of the Secretary's house, it was twilight, the remains of the day a pink and purple brushstroke across the horizon. He lived in a massive, three-story, red brick townhouse with white window trim and black shutters. It thrust upward with carefully crafted dignity, surrounded by weeping willows and giant oaks. It perfectly signaled the status of its occupants.

"How much does a place like this cost in Georgetown?" I asked Aislinn as we climbed out of the cab.

"Easily a million," she replied, her face glowing with anticipation.

The walkway leading to the front door was lined with softly lit lanterns and a variety of flowers. The doorbell chimed quietly but clearly, followed immediately by the smooth opening of the door. A black man in white jacket and pants stood to the side, one arm on the door and the other extended outwards to take our coats.

"Welcome," he said, smiling.

Aislinn took his cue and dumped her coat in his arms, breezing past him into the marble foyer. I gave him mine and looked him in the eye and said, "Thanks."

He looked a little surprised at being acknowledged, obviously not used to people treating him as anything other than useful décor.

A man stepped out of a side room and opened his arms, calling out, "Aislinn!" She smiled and gave him a small, dignified hug. Then she turned towards me and said, "Mr. Secretary, this is Mark Christian."

"Ah, yes, the private detective! We've heard about you. Not working tonight I hope!" he said heartily, shaking my hand.

I laughed politely. "No, sir. Not tonight."

"None of that 'sir' stuff now," he offered cheerfully. "Call me 'Bob.'"

He was late middle-aged and in good shape. The hair was more grey than black, and overly sprayed in place. His dress was expensive casual, and his eyes gleamed with the easy confidence of a man used to getting what he wants. As he turned back to Aislinn, he gave her a hungry glance that took in the full length of her figure. It was done discreetly and quickly enough to maintain deniability.

It didn't bother me in the slightest, as she was beautiful beyond belief tonight in a perfectly fitting black dress. Her red hair spilled around her bare shoulders. Hell, he'd be nuts if he didn't notice. But it made me wonder if his motivations for being her mentor were completely professional. In any case, I had the sense that he had more than a few fantasies about what might happen on one of their business trips together.

"Bob" took us by the arm and into an elegant side room, stuffed with people drinking and talking. Within the space of a few minutes, I was introduced to two reporters, a congressman, a bunch of congressional aides, and high-level commerce staffers.

You could feel it as you talked to them, the attitude of people as commodities to be acquired or discarded, based on their monetary or political value. The best of them— the truly nice ones—were perfectly cordial and welcoming. But even with them, you could tell that they had to try to be nice and welcoming to someone they considered less than themselves. Their most natural stance was exclusion of such people, and they had to work at the opposite. In this world people had no intrinsic value in and of themselves, as the humanists and good-will religions would have us believe; they only had value by virtue of their position, influence, usefulness, and ability to make each other look good.

I was separated from Aislinn when she was pulled into a conversation with the Secretary and a congressman. I was grabbed by a couple of her younger, female co-workers, who drilled me for all the info they could get about my relationship with Aislinn.

"Do you really ride a motorcycle?"

"Where do you work out?"

"Have you proposed yet?"

"God," one of them said eventually, "Aislinn is so lucky. These Washington guys are the worst. All they care about is their damn careers. Remember Julie telling us about that guy she dated, the one who watched McLaughlin while they had sex!"

The girls all laughed.

"Are you serious?" I asked, thinking that she must be exaggerating.

"Absolutely. You have no idea, dear."

"They can't all be that bad," I said charitably.

"Yes, they can," the girls said in unison, laughing.

Aislinn appeared at my side and said, "Excuse me, girls. May I have my boyfriend back."

"Sure. We're done interrogating him, anyway."

"It was my pleasure," I said to them as Aislinn pulled me away.

We headed to the other side of the room where a group of young men stood in a circle, laughing. They were clean shaven, wore dress shirts and ties, and had the arrogant, expectant air of young men next in line to rule the world.

"Brad wants to meet you," Aislinn whispered in my ear as we made our way through the constellations of people.

"Sure. Isn't that the guy who wants to marry you?"

"Yep. I bet he wants to size you up," she said with a hint of resentment.

"No problem."

"Just brace yourself; he can be a real jerk."

"No problem."

Brad was a good-looking kid with a bratty air about him. Suspenders, power tie, and black hair slicked back, a la Gordon Gecko.

"Here he is, the boyfriend of the moment," Brad called out cheerfully as we approached. He was clearly working on a pretty good buzz as he slightly slurred the word "boyfriend."

"Mark, this is Brad," Aislinn said. "He's the chief aide to Senator Cianelli."

"As yes, Brad, *wanna-be* boyfriend of the moment," I said with equal cheerfulness.

Brad laughed it off, obviously not prepared for a comeback. He was clearly used to dealing with people who needed something from him, and were, therefore, more likely to put up with his shit.

I caught a couple of his friends smiling slightly, pleased to see him taken down a notch. The others looked affronted that someone of my station in life—or lack thereof— would so casually disrespect someone of their class.

Brad tried a different tactic; he started a conversation with Aislinn and his friends and pointedly ignored me.

"So Aislinn, when are you going to come work for us? You know, it's much more exciting on the Hill," he said. And so it went on for a good fifteen minutes while I stood sipping a glass of Merlot and daydreaming.

"It'll never pass unless they get Langford on board."

"What does the Secretary think, Aislinn? He's got the President's ear."

"Targeted trade! It was clear as a fucking bell in the provisions, but apparently those fucking protestors don't read."

"Look at that bastard Jewell over there kissing the congressman's ass. As if he has a fucking chance in hell of getting something good for the Post."

Just as I was getting ready to make a break for the bathroom, a voice rang out, saying, "Ladies and Gentleman, dinner is ready."

The table was magnificent, seating twenty beneath a sparkling chandelier. I sat next to Aislinn in the middle of the table. Brad was directly across from us, the Secretary was at the head of the table, the congressman at his right. And the conversation continued as before.

"So they send one of their people to ask for help after they've been hiding losses for years in dummy companies, as if there is something that I can do!"

"It was spun a bit to the right in a pathetic attempt at triangulation. But if you think that's what he really believes...."

"The Chinese know full well we're not going to budge on that point."

I wondered how much of it was designed specifically to be heard by the reporters at the table. In any case, I was amazed at how comfortable and familiar they were with the political personages. Clearly, the media and political elites were merged somewhat in a common social circle. I figured there must be some unspoken understanding that anything heard at these tables was unreportable, at least from the standpoint of quoting anyone directly.

I was completely at peace, quietly eating my catered pasta dish and soup, listening and learning about this new culture. Aislinn would squeeze my hand occasionally to let me know she was still with me or smile and whisper something in my ear. I was impressed with her easy confidence in this arena and unerring ability to speak with a perfect blend of deference, knowledge, and self assurance. I could also see that she had a way of complimenting people without it seeming fake or forced. She was clearly capable of going far in this world.

The Secretary, concerned that I was not being included in the conversations, decided to screw things up by singling me out for attention. I would have been perfectly content to have been ignored all evening. "So, Mr. Christian. Aislinn tells us you're a private detective."

The noise at the table died down, and most eyes turned towards me.

"Yes."

"Working on any interesting cases? If not, I've got a couple of colleagues I'd like you to follow around," he said, smiling wickedly.

Most of the people at the table laughed politely.

"Right now I'm working on a murder case."

"Oh, my gosh! Sounds exciting," he exclaimed.

"It has its moments."

Aislinn said, "Mark was in the Marines before he became an investigator. He served with distinction in Iraq and Somalia. He won the Purple Heart and two Silver Stars." She was clearly trying to establish my credentials and ease my entree into group acceptance. To establish my worthiness to be here.

"A war hero!" said the Secretary of Commerce. "Good for you, young man. I'm pleased to see that our country can still produce men capable of her defense."

"You got beat in Somalia, didn't you?" Brad interjected, a look of false compassion on his face. It was clear he resented any positive attention going towards his rival for Aislinn's affections.

"No, we did not," I said softly but firmly. "Somalia was lost right here in Washington after the administration got cold feet and pulled us out. They sent us into battle without the tools to get the job done, with ridiculous rules of engagement. Even so, we won every firefight we engaged in."

There was an embarrassed silence. It was obvious that most of the people at the table had supported the Clinton policy on Somalia.

"Well perhaps there were larger issues you didn't understand," Brad said, smiling.

"Perhaps. But I do understand that you don't send America's sons and daughters into combat without the tools to get the job done, or tie one hand behind their backs in a fight with overly restrictive rules of engagement. And I understand that when you put your military in harm's way, you don't cut and run at the first sign of trouble. There are people out there who mean us harm, who took our withdrawal from Somalia without accomplishing our mission as a sign of weakness. In the long run, it may embolden terrorists and rogue states and lead to far more loss of life."

"Well in any case, we all appreciate that you've served your country as a soldier," Brad said, changing the subject. "Sun Tzu had that interesting quote about the kind of man to use as a soldier—I can't quite remember it. Never mind; it's not important," Brad said, waving his hand in dismissal.

He knew it, and at least a couple of people at the table did. I could tell from their warning looks to him. What they didn't know was that I also knew it. *As you would not use a rusty nail to build a house, do not use a good man to be a soldier.* I was tempted to say it out loud to expose his rudeness, but for Aislinn's sake, I let it pass. I didn't want to escalate things and embarrass her in the process.

"Where did you go to school, Mr. Christian?" This time the question was from an older lady far down the table. The wife of one of the personages, but I wasn't sure who.

"I never did go to college."

"Oh, really?"

"Really. I never wanted it to get in the way of my learning."

About half the table laughed, and the other half looked shocked or confused.

One old man at the end of the table clearly got it. He gazed at me sharply with interest and an appreciative smile. "I think I know what the young man means," he said. "Most of the important learning we do in life is out of school. But a fancy degree can sometimes delude you into thinking that you know more than you really do."

"Well," Brad interjected, "I wish someone had told me that before I went to Harvard! It could have saved me a lot of time and money!"

Several other people nodded, smiling slightly.

The Secretary of Commerce nodded at the old man and said, "Mr. Christian, this is my father Charles. He, like you, is a veteran and rebel. Why, we must have moved twenty times when I was growing up while he chased various dreams. Only he would argue against the value of higher education. I have a feeling that you two are cut from the same cloth."

"I'm not against higher education," I replied. "I'm merely suggesting that there are other paths to learning and wisdom that are equally valuable."

That more diplomatic but truthful stating of my position seemed to mollify everyone, so I took the opportunity to change the subject. I turned to the Secretary's father and asked, "Which service were you in, sir?"

"I was in the Army Air Corps during World War II. Flew B-24's over Germany," he said with pride.

"Rough duty," I said.

"It was, indeed."

"And I was in Vietnam," the congressman said, "slogging around the A Shau valley with an APC unit. We spent a lot of time stuck in mud." He was a fifteen year veteran of the House and important member of some trade committee, hence his invitation tonight and placement at the table.

"Stuck in the mud! I like that," one of the reporters said. "Sounds like a good description of the whole Vietnam experience."

There was general agreement with that point and then the conversation went back to politics. And I went back to being happily ignored.

After dinner we broke up into groups. Aislinn was chatting with some of her co-workers, and another group centered around the Secretary, who heatedly discussed hot issues on the Hill.

I was surrounded by a small cluster of people, wanting to hear more about my profession. I was used to this; it was a magnet for interest and questions, so I entertained them with some of my better stories, careful to make them vague enough to protect client confidentiality. Normally I never talk much about what I do, my natural inclination being toward reticence. But I was playing it up a bit tonight, knowing that if I made a favorable impression, it would reflect well on Aislinn. I tended to be too direct to be diplomatic, but I had great material for stories and intended to make the most of it.

I was mid-way into a bizarre story about an embezzler and his relationship with his pet donkey that had a great elements of danger and hilarity when one of the ladies interrupted me by asking, "How do you do that kind of work? Aren't you afraid of dying?"

"No, it's giving in to fear that I worry about. Fear will kill you quicker than anything. When you live in fear, you could live to be ninety and be dead every minute of it."

"But doesn't that lead to recklessness with your own life and maybe others," one of the men asked.

"It can if used unwisely. But part of the fear you face is the fear of what people will think if you walk away from a fight, when walking away is the wisest thing to do or when it reduces the risk of harm coming to innocents. Fear of death is the least of what I'm talking about; it's the fear of what other people think that kills most of us."

There seemed to be general agreement with that point, and so I went back to the story. When I finished, the group exploded in hysterical laughter.

Aislinn looked at me from the other side of the room and gave me a proud smile. Having accomplished my goal and done my duty as her boyfriend, I then steered the conversation away from myself by asking other people questions about their lives.

Later on Brad broke into our group and began to hold forth on the *demise of higher culture*. At one point he asked me, in an obviously patronizing tone, "Do you listen to much classical music, Mr. Christian?" The barely discernable sneer on his face clearly indicated his certainty that I didn't.

I took a deep breath. I had been polite all night as this guy threw various veiled, patronizing, elitist barbs my way. But enough is enough.

"Haydn is not one of my favorites," I responded easily, referring to the composer currently being played on the stereo, "with the exception of his trumpet concerto in E flat, the second movement. I have some good personal associations with that piece. But overall, I prefer jazz. It's more often the product of brilliant, self-educated musicians living authentic lives. As opposed to classical, which was created by the pampered, kept musicians of the privileged class. I have little respect for men who whore themselves to more powerful men." I held his eyes as I said it, the challenge out on the table.

He nodded twice, his face turning red with anger. The people around us were deeply quiet, waiting for his response.

"Are you implying that anyone who works for a powerful man is a whore?!"

"No. Just the ones like you."

153

Brad stormed off, leaving the room. One of the reporters, who had been on the periphery of our group talking to a colleague, leaned towards us and chuckled, saying, "Nice job. That prick has had that coming to him for years."

Much later, on the ride home in a beat-up old taxi, Aislinn looked quietly concerned.

"What's wrong?"

"Brad complained to the Secretary about you. Said you were rude to him and that he was *deeply disappointed.* Brad was there for a specific reason, Mark, and it's not because we enjoy his company. We need Senator Cianelli's support on a bill coming before the Senate, and Brad's advice will have a major influence on what the Senator decides. Brad is perfectly capable of seeing that we're denied, just to pay us back for being humiliated at the Secretary's party. What did you say to him?"

"I, um, ... called him a whore."

"You did what?!"

"Aislinn, that asshole was insulting me all night long with patronizing comments and veiled insults. I was patient with it for hours, but at some point, you have to let someone know that enough is enough. So I came back at him. I swear, if he is any indication of the type of people you have to deal with at work... I don't know how you do it."

"Now your patronizing me," she said angrily. "Do you think that there are no lower-class assholes? So we've got them in the upper classes, too. What's the big surprise? Anywhere you have people, you have assholes."

"Ok, then, but would you react this way if I put one of those 'lower class assholes' in his place like I did that sniveling snake Brad? I don't think so. If he wasn't some senator's aide, you wouldn't be this upset."

"Yes, you're right. I have to work with these people. And we need Brad to get this bill passed, and he may one day be able to offer me a job, get me out of the bureaucracy and into more interesting work. In Washington if you take on every asshole your going to end up taking on half the town. Nothing would ever get done. Not all of us have jobs where we can fly solo and speak our mind every minute of the day. YOU are the arrogant one, looking down on the poor rest of us who don't go through life with your perfect, marvelous integrity."

"Hey, I never said I have perfect integrity. It's not possible to have perfect integrity. But I tried to ignore that prick for hours, and he wouldn't give it up. Would you have respected me if I had let him insult me all evening and didn't do anything about it?"

"Yes, I would," she replied. "Don't you get it? Brad hates you because he knows you are a better man, and he can't stand that thought. Isn't it enough that you know that you are the better man? Couldn't you let him play his games and leave it at that?"

"I'm sorry if this causes problems for you Aislinn, but I come from a different universe. In my universe you don't tolerate a disrespectful, tactless, arrogant person's abuse just because you need something from him."

"Fair enough. Maybe that's one of the reasons I'm attracted to you. Maybe on some level I long for the simplicity of your moral stance," she said. "But my universe is much more complicated. Sometimes in my reality when you don't tolerate someone's crap, far worse things happen than getting your pride hurt. We're supporting this trade bill because we think it will help a lot of people. Make their jobs more secure and even create jobs. Putting up with a jerk like Brad is a small price to pay to achieve that higher goal."

I was silent, slightly chastened. "I'm sorry hon. I can see that. But remember that I didn't know all this going into the party. It would of helped to be clued in."

"I shouldn't have to tell you not to call a senator's aide, or anyone else for that matter, a whore at a party! Oh, and here's another beauty. You sit at a table with distinguished graduates of Harvard, Yale, Stanford, and put down the value of higher education. Speaking of tactless. Then you give everyone a lecture about how the administration screwed up in Somalia, when some of the most important collaborators in that policy where sitting right there."

I paused, then said meekly, "But I told a really good story about an embezzler and his donkey."

Aislinn's lip began to tremble as she fought to restrain her laughter. Then she burst out laughing and said, "Oh, God, what am I going to do with you? And don't make me laugh! I need to be angry with you right now."

The tension diffused a bit, I sat back and thought about what tonight meant for my relationship with Aislinn. I was nuts about her, but it was becoming increasingly clear that we were not compatible as lifetime partners. In the present I was an exciting adventure for her, a fantasy fulfilled before settling down to domesticity with some suitably conservative, successful, professional partner. The kind of guy she didn't have to explain defensively to her parents, who fits in at cocktail parties with the Secretary of Commerce and other high powered personages, and you can raise kids with and build a stable future. In the long term I was a dangerous wild-card, an aberration that threatened the achievement of her carefully constructed future: salutorian, Stanford Phi Betta Kappa, staff assistant to the Secretary of Commerce, and maybe some day Secretary? A home in Georgetown and two kids who go to the Ivy League by way of some prestigious private school. And likely, given the cycles of life, one of them a daughter, who will one day have a wild passionate fling of her own with a guy like me; if not a private detective, then a writer or artist or musician. Barely able to eke out a living, too nomadic or unstable to raise kids with, but dangerous and exciting and free. And maybe mom will look into her daughters eyes during that time and smile inwardly, remembering with secret pleasure the bad boy from her youth, while mouthing words of caution, *great to date but lousy to marry*. She will warn her daughter, and she will be right. But still glad that her daughter will live—really live—with true unrestrained joy and freedom, if only for a little while. And knowing that it is no less precious for not lasting.

- 16 –

I tailed Fredericks day after day as he followed the same routine: out of the house by 8:30 in the morning, walk to the metro, take the red line to Union Station, walk to the Government Printing Office, arriving anywhere from fifteen to thirty minutes late. He would leave at exactly five pm from work, reverse the pattern, and spend the rest of the night locked in his house, probably in a dope nod.

The only change in his pattern started a couple of days ago, when he'd started to cop dope on the street with greater frequency. When I'd first started tailing him, he'd hadn't been buying heroin at all. All of a sudden, he began buying four times a day from various street dealers in his neighborhood.

My guess was that he had run out of the high-grade heroin I'd found in his house and was getting by on street dope until he could re-up on the good stuff. It was a conclusion born out by the books on heroin addiction that I'd been reading, in an attempt to make sense of what I was seeing.

According to one book, the heroin bought on the streets of the inner cities was always the poorest quality, being up to seventy percent 'cut.' To cut your supply means to add any white powder that looks like heroin, so that it won't be noticed by the buyer. That way you have more to sell, and make more money. The dealers cut heroin with quinine, vitamin B-12, meat tenderizer, and baking soda. The average addict injects that crap into their veins four to eight times a day.

With street dope, the book said, it was almost impossible to overdose, given the low percentage of heroin in any given bag. It was also cheap, averaging about $20 a hit. However, the garbage that it had been cut with collapsed the veins, toxified the body to the point that it turned the user a sickly grey, and damaged all the major organs, especially the liver. Once all the veins in the arms collapsed, the heroin addict progressed to injecting into the veins of the hands and feet, and eventually the groin, neck, and forehead.

The purer heroin, like the China white I'd found in Fredericks drawer, did less damage to the body, but there was a far greater risk of dying from an overdose. Plus, it created a monster habit that was far harder to kick and cost the kind of money that only rock stars, actors, and the idle rich could afford.

So I returned to the question that kept me tailing Fredericks day after day; where was he getting the money to afford China white? His government salary? No way. He wasn't getting the money from dealing either; I was sure of that from tailing him fourteen hours a day. He was strictly a buyer. What was he into? How did it tie into the murder of Eric Jones, if at all? Was I solving the wrong case?

The sky threatened rain with charcoal grey clouds that streamed by in an unbroken ceiling. The wind picked up, its sound barely perceptible over the din of the traffic. I sat in a coffee shop on North Capitol Street, across from the government printing shop. I'd been there for over five hours, and was beginning to get curious looks from the employees as they came around to bus the tables.

Tailing someone was monumentally boring work and strewn across the table before me were the things that I'd brought to ease the pain; my Walkman, a few jazz tapes, a book, and a pack of cigarettes. Occasionally, I looked up from my book and out the plate glass window at the Government Printing Office. An amazing volume of people had been going in and out of it all day long, and I was nervous that Fredericks might slip out while I was reading. I was willing to take the chance though, because a person could stare at a doorway for only so long. I tried for the first hour or so, sipping coffee and gazing at the huge archway with double doors beneath, until my eyes started to cross, and it felt like I was slipping into a coma. After a couple of weeks of this, I understood why many private eyes worked with a partner or firm. It would be heaven to have someone to alternate shifts with, instead of having to do it all myself.

The only thing I'd noticed today was many of the employees at the Government Printing Office took long, frequent cigarette breaks, and spent a lot of money at the corner hot dog stand. Your tax dollars at work. Of course, I couldn't blame them; if I worked there, I'd probably be finding an excuse to go outside every hour, too. Fredericks had not yet been among them, probably because his breaks consisted of shooting dope in the bathroom.

A bus rolled to a stop in front of the coffee shop, hissing as its pneumatic doors opened. It blocked my view across the street. I waited impatiently, trying to stare through it while the passengers embarked. Finally the doors closed, and the bus pulled out into the traffic, cutting off two cars and trailing a cloud of exhaust smoke. I looked across the street and just caught sight of an unmarked police car pulling to the curb in front of the Government Print Shop. It was easy to recognize from the extra antennae mounted on the rear hood, and the unusual tags. Were the cops onto Fredericks, or was it a coincidence? I'd know within a couple of minutes.

Fredericks walked out of the Government Printing Office, holding a faded blue backpack, which he clutched tightly to his chest. He walked straight to the police cruiser and got in. I frantically stuffed my Walkman, tapes, book and cigarettes into a bag, threw a twenty on the table, and sprinted out the door of the coffee shop.

Just as I reached my bike, the cruiser pulled into the rush-hour traffic on North Capitol, cutting off the on-coming cars. It was done with the casual arrogance of someone used to having people make way. That confirmed it. Definitely cops. I put on my helmet, kick-started the Triumph, and pulled in behind them, careful to stay six or seven cars back.

My first thought was that the police had beaten me to it, had nailed Fredericks, and that he had just turned himself in. But when the cruiser headed out of the city on 395 I knew, with a surge of adrenaline, that I was wrong.

They took the exit for National Airport, and I followed, afraid of losing them, but resisting the urge to close the gap. We went through Crystal City, over a small bridge, and around the circular road in front of the old terminal at National Airport, its right lane jammed with parked taxi's and cars dropping off passengers.

I continued to follow well behind as we got on the access road to the newer terminal. The road twisted, merged with other roads, and split without warning, and I began to wonder if the designer had been dropping acid when he laid this out.

The cruiser pulled into an exclusive, restricted parking lot next to the new terminal. It was the place where the congressmen and senators parked when leaving on their lobbyist-paid junkets and visits to the home state. There was no way I'd be able to get in there, so I pulled into the general parking area adjacent to it, carefully looking for a space where I would be hidden from view, but could still see into the restricted lot. I finally settled on a spot next to a concrete divider and a silver minivan that tried to look modern and sleek, but was just ugly.

It had taken an hour and a half to drive the twenty or so miles from the city to National Airport, because southbound routes out of the District at rush hour have some of the worst traffic in the world. As such, my legs were cramped and stiff as I got off of the Triumph.

The sun was nearly down, lingering on the horizon in a blaze of red and yellow and vermilion, and the sky overhead was nearly dark. Nearby was the vast block of the newer terminal, with jets parked against the black, tendriled arms of the walkways. The air had that unique, oddly pleasing, smell of jet fuel and shook with the distant sound of planes taking off and landing. I could feel my soul settle in an indescribable way at the recognition, the immense familiarity that these sights and sounds evoked. An airport, for the military veteran of the last quarter century, was a crossroads of memory, redolent with the images of a thousand departures, feelings, and good-byes. It is to the modern military man what the train station was to the veteran of World War II.

In a flash of memory, I was taken back six years to an evening much like this when I'd walked in a shadowed line of figures, weighted down with equipment, towards a distant plane, waiting to carry us to Saudi Arabia. We'd been on round-the-clock alert for the last forty-eight hours and had finally gotten the *word*, and had saddled up, burying an avalanche of mounting feelings under the dull routine of familiar rituals: weapons checks, gear checks, helping other guys get on their seventy pound packs.

There had been a moment as I'd walked out onto the tarmac and cleared the lights of the terminal, the vast bulk of the C-5 Galaxy—the largest military transport plane in the world—and Hussein's million man army looming closer with each step, plodding forward with the dull insistence of obligation, inhaling deeply the smell of jet fuel, when I'd looked up, and overhead shone the infinite beauty of the stars—Orion, Cappella, Cirrus, Andromeda—and I'd been overtaken by a quiet certitude, an overwhelming wonder, and an indescribable yearning that was both a question and an answer, a beginning and an ending. The kind of moment where one could see with the eyes of the soul, that monks and mystics fast and slave and sacrifice a lifetime for. An eternal now, a moving shimmer, a glimmer of peace fleeting, and then the universe dwindled again to the cut of the pack straps against my shoulder, the ache in my wrist and feet, the cold feel of the rifle.

J.D. Miller

Living in their pools they soon forget about the sea was a line from one of my favorite songs, and it perfectly describes how many people live their lives, oblivious to the transcendent beauty around them and the possibilities of expanded consciousness.

In that moment I saw the extent that I had structured my life around achieving those moments; through cultivation of inner freedom, self-determination, the obsessive pursuit of personal growth and intrinsic values. Through the refusal to live an anxiety-based life, unfettered by the crushing weight of fear.

All of this ran through my mind in a lightning flash of intuition, more felt than reasoned, and then I was fully back on the tarmac at National Airport, leaning to the right in order to see around the minivan and into the next parking lot.

The police cruiser wasn't there; it had gone through a gate and parked a little ways out onto the tarmac, about twenty-five feet from a private jet.

Fredericks and two D.C. cops got out of the police cruiser and stood next to it, waiting. Fredericks was still clutching the backpack tightly, looking thin and insubstantial next to the two bulky cops.

Then the door to the jet swung down in an arc, coming to rest on the tarmac. A man came down the steps. He was Asian, with an expensive suit, no tie, and long black hair tied in a ponytail. He was carrying two envelopes.

It was a moment of decision. I could stay put and watch the exchange with no guarantee that I would ever be able to find out what had happened or why. It was the safe, practical decision, of course, but I could

164

spend the rest of my life watching them exchange envelopes and bags and never learn a damn thing of substance. The other choice was to stir things up and see what came to the surface, at considerable risk to my life.

I slipped over the concrete divider and crawled towards the tarmac, hidden from view by the parked cars. I made it to the tarmac in good time and stood up and walked out towards the police car.

Fredericks and the two cops had their backs to me, but the guy in the suit spotted me immediately. He pointed at me and said something to the other three, and they turned around to look. Fredericks looked at me blankly for a moment before recognizing me. He shouted a warning.

The Asian guy had the most presence of mind, and started to draw his 9mm, but I'd been practicing the fast draw for years and had my gun centered on his chest by the time that his was half-way out. He knew I had him and froze in mid-draw.

"Put it down."

He opened his hand without moving the arm, and the pistol dropped to the tarmac.

"You, too," I said to the cops.

They complied.

"Stand over there, away from the guns." I motioned with my head toward my side of the police cruiser.

They did so; the two cops and the Asian guy calm, Fredericks looking like he had just shit his pants.

"Fredericks, how have you been? Remember me?"

The three others turned to him, and the Asian guy asked in good English, with only the faintest trace of an accent, "You know this man?"

"Yeah," Fredericks said, his voice quavering. "He's a private detective hired by Eric Jones' mother."

"Throw the envelopes and backpack towards me," I said.

They made no move to do so, and one of the cops said, "You don't know what you're doin' man. Walk away before it's too late."

"Shut up," the Asian man said with an easy authority. He turned towards me and held up an envelope. "This is ten thousand dollars. Please consider it payment for your time and trouble and go on your way."

"Why should I?"

"Because if you do not, we will kill you." I'd heard that a lot lately.

"I'm just bright enough to know that we're past that point already. You're going to try to kill me either way. So hand over the fucking bag and the two envelopes, and then I'll go on my way."

The other three looked wide-eyed at the Asian guy. He nodded calmly. They threw the stuff toward me, and I picked it all up with one hand, not taking my eyes off them.

Then I shot out two tires on the poice cruiser, stuffed their weapons in the backpack, walked to my motorcycle, and drove home.

- 17 -

Passport, United States of America. It had been instantly recognizable the moment I'd pulled it out of Fredericks' backpack, with its small navy-blue cover, official seal, and indented serial number. I opened it up and flipped through it. The pages were blank. I looked inside the backpack and counted six more passports. Next I checked the envelopes. In one I found twenty thousand dollars in cash, and in the other I found twenty bags of what looked like high-grade heroin.

I lit a cigarette, leaned back in my office chair, and thought about what I'd found. Now that I had most of the pieces of the puzzle, it wasn't hard to put together. Fredericks works for the Government Printing Office. One of the many things that they print is passports. So someone is paying him to steal a small number of them on a regular basis. In return, they pay Fredericks in cash and high-grade heroin that he wouldn't be able to afford otherwise.

To ensure that the passports are delivered safely to the waiting courier, they have a couple of crooked cops on their payroll drive Fredericks to the airport. It's a good idea, guaranteeing Fredericks won't be found out on a routine traffic stop. In return, the two cops probably get a percentage of the twenty thousand dollars. Not bad for a couple of hours work, and the people behind this get a regular supply of real passports to use when coming into the country or forging false identities.

So it's likely that one day shortly before his death, Eric Jones—a supervisor at the Government Printing

Office—found out that passports were missing and started to look into it. Or maybe he caught Fredericks stealing passports and threatened to turn him into the police or fire him. Fredericks tells the people behind this that they are about to be blown, so they put out a hit on Eric, careful to make it look like a random drive-by shooting by a local drug crew, so the police wouldn't snoop around the Government Printing Office. It was a good plan, and it had worked—until now.

I rolled my desk chair over to a window and opened it. The sound of the katydids drifted in with the warm night air. I sat there a while, feet propped up on the windowsill, staring into the darkness. So what happens next? Whoever was behind this was certain to try to kill me in the near future, maybe tonight. They'd want to do me before I had a chance to go to the police or the Feds. Fredericks knew who I was, and from that they could easily find out where I lived.

I called Butch DeCarlo for advice. I got an admin assistant and the old "I'm sorry he's out of the office; would you like his voice mail?" line. Why does every office worker in the world say the same things in the same way? Just once I'd like to hear something like "He's been paroled," or "He ran out screaming." Anyway, I decided to try him at home, but after shuffling through the papers on my desk realized that I had lost his home number. So I jumped on my bike and headed for Fairfax. I had been to his place a couple of times for dinner and knew where he lived.

An hour later I was standing in front of a four-story, red brick apartment complex in Annandale, just off the beltway. Butch, like many younger people who work in the city, could not afford the astronomical cost of buying a house in the D.C. area, and so was forced to pay the slightly less astronomical cost of renting an apartment. Around here, a small two-bedroom, box house with no yard can cost you $300,000. If Butch's wife worked full time, they still might be able to get one, but they had made the decision that they wanted one of them home for at least the first five years of their child's life, so they had sacrificed the house and SUV and the leather furniture and probably any kind of costly vacation for the welfare of their child. You gotta respect that.

Butch's wife Debbie opened the door. She was short, with full curves in all the right places, long blond hair, and an adorable face.

"Deb!" I gave her a quick hug.

"Mark, what are you doing here?"

"Sorry for not calling. I lost your number. I need to talk to Butch about something."

"Who's that?" Butch's voice boomed from the kitchen.

"Guess! It's your perpetually single friend!" she answered, grinning at me.

"Mark!" Butch called out without hesitation. "Come on in!"

I found Butch hunched over a pot of boiling water, stirring the pasta they were having for dinner. He gave me a bone-crushing hug. He was so big that my face got lost in his chest, and everything went dark for a moment.

"I'm impressed," I said when we disengaged. "You're cooking dinner."

169

"Well, I don't do it often. Spaghetti is about all that Deb will let me cook. Everything else I screw up. Why don't you stay for dinner?"

"Thanks."

I went into the small living room where Debbie and the baby were watching an episode of "Barney." After watching it with them for a couple of minutes, I had a strange urge to pull my .45 and put a round into the center of the TV screen, but I restrained myself.

Deb quizzed me about my love life, which was an endless source of fascination for her, and I told her all about Aislinn. When she asked me if Aislinn and I were going to get married, and I said "I don't know," I was subjected to more questions and a disapproving statement or two about my reluctance to move quicker. She was a true "marriage missionary," who considered it her task in life to cajole those unfortunate single people she meets into a higher state of matrimonial grace.

At dinner I entertained Debbie with stories of Butch's antics in the Marine Corps, which she seemed to take as further proof of the need for her civilizing influence on him. She was probably right.

In the Marines his idea of a fun night had been to rip beer cans apart with his teeth and display the pieces with an immensely satisfied grin. Or knocking sailors out with one punch. It rarely took more than that, and he would often go through brief bouts of depression when it took two or—God forbid—three. The incidents would usually start with someone using foul language or making a disrespectful remark in front of a woman. Butch was psychotic about that. He considered the female species to be sacrosanct and would not tolerate anything other than absolutely proper, respectful behavior. God help the guy at a bar or in barracks, who was otherwise. Even implied disrespect could bring Butch's wrath.

One night at a bar, a guy at a table next to us was telling his friends that his new girlfriend liked to "swallow the salami—with mayo—if you know what I mean." Butch threw him through the front window.

Another time in barracks a new guy had looked at the picture of Butch's girlfriend hanging above his bunk and said, "She's hot; I wouldn't mind doing her." It took six of us to hold Butch down. The poor new guy hid in an ammo shed for the rest of the day and asked for a transfer the next week.

He and I became friends because I was the only guy who wasn't completely intimidated by him. That and a strong set of principles acceptable to Butch were the price of admission into his heart. Even our instructors in Recon were a bit wary, as one would be around a rabid dog. But as one of the few people who had delved beneath the surface and gotten to know him better, I had found him to be an absolutely loyal friend, faultlessly courageous, surprisingly thoughtful at times, with a broad streak of hidden gentleness that only came out with people he absolutely trusted. He was like a big, sweet, lovable Neanderthal. But Deb and fatherhood had forced him to evolve. Now he was at least up to Australopithecus.

As dinner progressed, the baby ignored us and slathered food all over her face and high chair. Hopefully, when she grew up, she would look like her mother. God help the pimply faced boys, who came by fifteen years from now to date her. If I'm still alive then—which, given my history, seems unlikely—I'll have to come by and chain Butch to a radiator so he doesn't end up in jail.

Later, while Debbie did the dishes, Butch and I went out onto the porch, broke out a couple of cigars, and caught up.

"How's the private eye thing going?"

"Rough right now. I'm struggling to pay the bills."

"Why don't you join the DEA? Get a steady paycheck. We could use someone with your skills."

"There's one big problem with that; I'm pro-legalization."

"Yeah. That would be a problem. I'll tell you though; we wonder ourselves sometimes. A million people in jail in this country, seventy percent of whom are in on drug charges, and we still haven't stopped it. Thousands of tons of drugs seized each year, and you can still buy drugs in most schools. On the other hand, I do believe that having them illegal does deter some people from trying drugs in the first place, and that the threat of incarceration helps motivate some people to clean up."

"I had dinner with Jay Mills a month ago," I said. "Do you remember him? You met him at that poker game at Greg's a couple years ago."

"Sure. Nice guy. A drug counselor, if I remember."

"Yeah. He was telling me about research that's been done in countries that have legalized drugs. They show an increase in addiction but a very large decrease in violent crime. And a lot of money freed up for treatment and prevention. It's not a perfect solution for sure, but shit, Butch, I've been in Southeast D.C. a lot recently, and you should see the wreckage the drug related violence has caused. It's unbelievable. We've got to try a new approach. Maybe it's time to treat it like a health problem, rather than a criminal justice problem."

"Hmmm," he responded noncommittally, the cigar smoke swirling around his head. "So what's up? Why'd you drop by tonight? I know it wasn't to debate legalization."

"I took a backpack from a guy I was tailing. In it was twenty thousand dollars and a whole bunch of heroin."

Butch nearly spit out his cigar. "What!"

"No shit. I need help buddy."

"Tell me everything from the beginning."

And so I told him about the Jones' case in general, my suspicions about Fredericks and tailing him to the airport, and the confrontation in front of the private jet.

"Did you get a tail number off the jet?"

"No. Didn't even think of it."

"The computer geeks at my office would need a tail number in order to find out anything quickly, so they probably wouldn't be much help. But I know a guy at the FBI who might be able to get the job done. A real wizard on the computer; name's Timmy Valentine. He's may be able to get you some information fast, and we *need it fast;* whoever you took that heroin from is going to be looking for you. Chances are they aren't planning a nice talk over a couple of beers, either. They'll be looking to take you out. I'll see if I can set up a meeting for first thing tomorrow."

- 18 -

The J. Edgar Hoover Building stands on E Street Northwest and is one of the most popular tourist attractions in D.C. Close to a half million people a year visit it, and it seemed like they were all there that day. It was absolutely swamped, and I was jostled several times as I made my way into the lobby.

My FBI escort for the day met me just inside the front entrance and gave me a skeptical once over. I didn't look like the blue-suited, clean-cut, all-American type they normally worked with. I was, in fact, a bit of a mess after an anxious, sleepless night in a hotel, bleary-eyed and on my second day without a shave. I was also on my second day wearing the same black leather jacket, motorcycle boots, and khaki pants.

"You're the private detective?" she asked. She was standard-issue bureau: short hair, fit, and very conservative looking. Rather attractive, actually, in a Republican kind of way.

"I am. Mark Christian," I said as I shook her hand. "I'm carrying. Is that a problem?"

"Jeez, yes. What have you got? Just tell me. Don't flash it, for God's sake."

".45 ACP."

"Let's go over to the side room and check it in. You'll get it back when you leave."

We got it done, and then she escorted me through numerous check points, locked doors, and down an elevator. We found Timmy Valentine working in a cramped cubicle in the basement of the building that looked like every other bleak office space in the world.

The only way I would know I was in the FBI building was the fact that I had an armed escort, who probably had orders to shoot me if I did anything untoward. I glanced at her. To give us some privacy, she had kindly retreated to the far side of the room.

"Gimme a minute," was Timmy's only greeting when I tried to introduce myself. He is a thin wisp of a man, with a soft jaw and scattered air. The clothes were slapdash and faded, and his hair stuck up in the back. But his eyes were piercing, sharp with intelligence.

He was totally immersed in an incomprehensible page of computer code, scrolling up and down with lightening speed, occasionally adding or subtracting from a particular line.

I stood behind him while he worked and checked out his space. He had three letters of reprimand framed and hanging from his cubicle walls. A rebel who takes pride in his mischief. My kind of guy. I looked at one letter more closely, and it was chastising him in nice official language for his "inappropriate dress not befitting an employee of the Federal Bureau of Investigations." I chuckled. *You and me both*, I thought. Another letter took him to task for "unauthorized access of classified data without due process." Well, I definitely had the right guy.

Timmy was typing like a madman now, adding lines of code with the speed of a secretary taking dictation. Then he stopped abruptly, threw his hands up in the air, and yelled, "Done!"

He turned to me with a grin, and said, "Check this out. It's for a girl I'm after."

A couple of more clicks and it was up on his monitor and running. It opened up with ornate, scrolling text that said "*One Reason Why You Should Date Timmy Valentine: He's a Great Dancer.*" Then it dissolved into a clip of Fred Astaire dancing with Ginger Rogers, with Timmy's head superimposed on Fred's body. As they spun and stepped with an easy grace, Tim's face grinned and winked at the camera. It was incredible. The lighting on his face even matched the movie's. Then it faded and became John Travolta, doing his famous solo dance in Saturday Night Fever, again with Timmy's face superimposed.

I was laughing hysterically, especially during the splits, and my FBI escort was peeking over my shoulder, trying to see what the fuss was about.

"Jeez, Timmy," she said. "Some of us in the Bureau actually work for a living. Is this how you spend your time?" But she smiled as she said it, clearly amused and amazed by what she had seen.

"You're just mad cause it's not for you."

"Yeah, right," she quipped, even more amused. Then she turned and went back to her spot on the other side of the room, making a call on the wall phone. Probably reporting Timmy. Here comes letter of reprimand number four.

"So what do you need? Butch said you've got a problem," Timmy said.

"I need to find the owner of a private jet that took off from National Airport yesterday. I don't have a tail number or any other identifying information. I also need to know what the owner might be into, illegally speaking."

"Is that all?" he said sarcastically. But his eyes gleamed. I could tell he was looking forward to the challenge.

"You love this shit, don't you?" I asked as he began to hack into the National Airport database.

"I do. It's like being God. You can go anywhere and see anything. You can alter someone's reality with a keystroke. Information is power, and this is where you get the information."

"Any ethical qualms?"

"Not really," he said absently as he typed away. "Most of what I do is sanctioned by the U.S. government. The stuff that isn't is always done toward a good end. I have rules I follow. When people ask me to do things that are not toward a good end, I just say no. Probably why I haven't been promoted in three years."

"What about the right to privacy?"

"Privacy," he said laughing, turning around to face me. "Privacy is a moot point, my friend. How can you protect a right that no longer exists? The NSA records every email and phone call made in the U.S. Many, if not most, companies read their employees' e-mails. Every time you go to an ATM, make a purchase with a credit card, get a drivers license, or make a health insurance claim, you send all kinds of information to databases that many people can easily access. Hidden cameras film you when you go into a department store, apartment building, or convenience store. When you drive through a toll booth, it photographs and stores your license plate numbers...."

"Point taken," I said, interrupting his diatribe. "It's still a little scary, though."

"You don't know the half of it," he muttered as he turned back to work. He continued for over an hour, during which time I stared at the ceiling.

"Here we go," he said finally. "The arrival and departure logs for private jets at National. The only one registered for the day and time you were there was a Gulfstream IV, tail number 63215J. Owner listed as a limited liability company. LLC's are red flags for people trying to be invisible. Origination point was listed as Singapore. Now let me see if I can trace this LLC to someone."

Timmy went back to hacking, and I stared at the ceiling some more. When that got boring, I stared at the back of Timmy's head. He had the beginnings of a bald spot, and I tried to predict the rate of expansion. I flipped through a trade magazine for high end computer users, chatted with my FBI escort, twirled a pen between my fingers, scratched my ass, went to the bathroom, hummed a U2 tune (until Timmy asked me to *please please shut the fuck up so I can concentrate*), tapped my feet, worried about getting shot, fantasized about what my escort would look like in a teddy, worried about getting shot, and wandered among the cubicles until, finally, Timmy called me over.

"The owners of the jet," he said, "are the new big players in the international heroin trade. Their name is the Red Shield. They're based in Singapore, and they ship the product coming out of the golden triangle all around the world. They're protected by the Malasayian government, because they present themselves as anti-communists and provide aid to the government troops fighting in the north of the country. But it's mainly a front to keep the government off their back."

I thanked Timmy profusely and used his phone to call Butch. Butch promised to start an investigation into Red Shield's role in stealing passports and put the word out on the street that the DEA would take it personally if anything bad happened to me. He doubted that it would do any good, but he'd try, anyway.

I spent the night in a motel in the middle of nowhere, sleeping in fits and starts that were more frustrating than restful. At four a.m. I gave up and drove into the city. My plan was to grab Fredericks early in the morning and see if I could get him to talk some more. How I would do this was beyond me, but at least it enabled me to do *something.* Passive hiding is not my style.

The gold Lexus parked in front of Fredericks' place immediately started my adrenaline pumping, because I remembered the D.C. detective, who had investigated Eric Jones's murder, had told me that a witness saw the shots come from a gold Lexus. Were they meeting with Fredericks to plan the hit on me?

I sat staring at Fredericks' front door for ten minutes before I got my answer. Two loud booms sounded from inside the house, and before I knew what I was doing, I had drawn my .45 and started across the street. The front door opened, and three black men piled out of the house and started towards the Lexus. Two had nines and the third carried a smoking Mossberg shotgun. They spotted me coming towards them, and it was on.

The two with pistols started popping off shots at me, and I went down on one knee, bringing my gun to bear. I could hear the supersonic screech as the bullets split the air around my head. I opened up and hit the nearest guy in the belly. He was lifted to his toes by the impact and stumbled two steps backward before going down. I must have hit an artery because blood was already spraying out of the wound as he fell.

The other two ducked down behind the Lexus.

I crouched lower and stayed put, waiting. Timed slowed, and I felt myself settle into a concentration that was razor sharp and absolute.

The guy hiding behind the rear hood of the Lexus started to come up to take a shot. In actuality, it was probably a half a second, but it seemed like an eternity as I watched first the top of his head, then his two wild, fearful, frantic eyes rise from behind the trunk of the Lexus.

By the time his arm and pistol started to appear, I was firing, the first shot missing just a hair to the left of his head. I corrected and put the next shot right into the middle of his face. It disappeared in an explosion of red mist, and he was blown backwards out of sight.

In virtually the same instant, the guy with the shotgun popped up from behind the front hood, snapped off a shot, and ducked back down.

I saw the sun flare of the muzzle flash and felt a hammer blow on my left thigh as I was knocked down backwards. Immediately I jumped back to my feet and started backing up, firing rapidly into the front hood of the Lexus to keep my opponents head down. With two rounds remaining in my clip, I ducked down behind the engine block of a tan Toyota across the street.

I realized now that this last guy was the truly dangerous one. The other two were amateurs. He had the presence of mind and ruthlessness to let his partner came up first, waiting for me to swing my gun to the right to take him out. He then came up on the left an instant later, giving him the advantage for one quick shot. He was not one who took senseless chances,or charged forward blindly. He waited for the advantage. With that thought, I had a plan.

Still lying behind the Toyata, I slipped my second piece out of my ankle holster, a six-shot, snub-nose .357 magnum. I flipped off the safety and put it in my right hand. I transferred the .45 to my left and jumped up, firing the remaining two rounds in the .45 across the street at the Lexus until the cartridge emptied, and the loud click of my trigger echoed into the street. As I'd thought, that encouraged him to come up to take a shot at me, right into the face of my .357.

My first shot hit his right shoulder and spun him around. Amazingly, he did not go down or drop the shotgun. My second shot hit his wrist and blew his hand off, the shotgun spinning away with it. I had been aiming for his chest, but with a snub nose cannon like the .357, it was hard to be accurate at distances over ten yards. Blood had just started to spray like water from a hose from his amputated wrist when my third shot hit him square in the chest. He flew backwards 5 feet as if yanked by some giant hand, coming to rest on his back in Fredericks yard, his chest smoking.

- *19* –

I woke up in the hospital, riding one hell of a morphine high. It felt like being wrapped in warm cotton, floating on a sea of serenity. I gingerly tried to raise my head to look around, but was flooded with a peaceful lassitude that didn't make it seem worth the effort, so instead turned inward and merged with the ebb and flow of opiate-induced pleasure.

A while later—I'm not sure how long—I managed to look around. There was another bed to my left. In it was a man in his late 50's, watching a TV that angled down from a wall mount. He wore an oxygen mask and stared blankly at a deodorant commercial. It was clearly implying that anyone who did not use their product was stinky and sexually unappealing, and that anyone who did would date hordes of supermodels. Our hospital room was stark and completely lacking in human warmth. It had a white tile floor and walls, heavy gray curtains, and a lot of medical equipment that softly beeped and hummed. Hospital standard décor.

I swung my head slowly to the right and saw a cop lounging in a chair next to my bed, looking at me from over the pages of a tattered magazine.

"Do you often read *Cosmo*?" I asked.

"Hey, lots of babes. Can't beat it. Especially when you get this kind of boring ass duty."

"You here to guard me or arrest me?"

"Maybe both. I'm not sure. All I know is that there are a lot of people who want to talk to you," he said, putting down the magazine. I listened as he used the phone next to my bed to call his shift supervisor and report my awakening. When finished, he said, "Your girlfriend is in the waiting room, taking a nap. You want me to go get her?"

"Yeah, thanks."

Aislinn walked in a couple of minutes later and leaned over to give me a kiss. She looked gorgeous as always, and she genuinely mouthed words of caring and concern, but there was something in her eyes, a barely discernible distance. A coldness deep within them that I'd never seen before. With a start, I realized that we had crossed some invisible line, that this was all too much for her, and she'd begun to pull away from me.

"I'm sorry to put you through this," I said. "This has just been a really bad year." I found myself explaining further, doing my best to convince her that this was an aberration and not my life. I did so despite knowing, on some deep level that I wouldn't admit even to myself, that it was not true. I didn't want to lose her, and desperation is the mother of denial.

She denied all concern and made a great effort to put me at ease, but I knew that the clock was ticking. I had a sense that it was probably just a matter of time before we broke up.

Aislinn is a nice person, so I knew that if she wanted to end things, she would wait till I was fully recovered. She still genuinely cared for me, so she probably wouldn't even end it outright. She would sabotage things unconsciously until our discord made the break that she couldn't bring herself to.

I couldn't blame her. My life was obviously too much for her, as it would be for most normal people.

Even most cops never shoot their guns in the course of their careers. In the last two weeks alone, I'd gotten a concussion in a fight, killed two men and been shot myself. I felt myself begin to slide downwards into a profound melancholy.

She stayed by my side and held my hand throughout the interview with the police.

I was questioned by Lt. Welton, who I had met at the beginning of this case. He was still the primary police investigator in the Eric Jones murder and still a sour-looking bastard. I told him everything, except the breaking and entering into Frederick's house. No sense asking for trouble.

He told me everything that happened after I passed out. The cops and EMTs had arrived in force. A rookie saw the guy I shot in the face and had promptly begun throwing up. There was nothing left but a gaping hole from mouth to forehead, and brain matter had splattered everywhere.

As Lt. Welton made some lame comment about how bad a .45 can fuck you up at close range, Aislinn made an excuse and walked out of the room. Welton checked her out in passing and shrugged, clearly not understanding what the problem was.

I called him an ignorant fuck-head, and he let it pass with a second shrug.

The guy I had shot in the stomach had survived by stuffing his shirt into his abdominal cavity to stop the bleeding. The last guy I killed had already been identified as Ronnie "Elmer" White, a notorious killer for hire, who had done jobs for dealers all over the city. He had gotten his nickname from those cartoons where Elmer Fudd hunts Bugs with a shotgun, our

"Elmer's" weapon of choice. He was suspected in at least nine execution-style killings. Welton went on to say that he had almost got him for one of the killings, but his main witness disappeared and had never been seen since.

Fredericks was found dead in his living room, splayed out on his couch with his chest shredded from two shotgun blasts: the Asian drug operation cleaning up loose ends.

The guy I shot in the stomach was on another floor of the hospital under 24 hour guard. He was singing in order to get a plea bargain and avoid prosecution for first-degree murder. He was claiming to be just the driver for Elmer's jobs (bullshit), and had fingered him for the murder of Eric Jones. He said that Fredericks had asked for the hit and had refused to give the reason, except to vaguely claim that Eric had discovered something he shouldn't.

Welton then told me that a DEA agent—my friend Butch DeCarlo—had called him and told him what Eric Jones had discovered: passports were missing at the Government Printing Office, and the inventory altered to hide their theft. The Eric Jones' murder case was being closed as solved.

The shootout had made the local news on all three networks, which was how my girlfriend and the DEA had discovered where I was. Speaking of which, both the DEA and FBI would be in to interview me later. The FBI wanted to go into the Government Printing Office and investigate the hell out of the place, to find out how this could have happened. The DEA wanted to look further into the Asian drug operation that was behind all this. IAD would also be by later to interview me; they wanted to know more about the two cops who had escorted Fredericks to National Airport.

Welton finished by thanking me for taking "some real scumbags who were wasting the oxygen that the rest of us could be breathing" off the street, then he walked out.

My doctor came in next. She was fairly young, petite, and very attractive in her own way. Not a conventional beauty by any means, but sexy as hell.

"Well, we're finally up," she said.

"Yes."

"I'm Dr. Dambroski. I did the work on your leg."

"Thanks."

"Sure," she said coolly, not looking up. She was reading my chart. After a pause she finished and said, "Well, Mr. Christian, according to your x-rays, you've had six broken bones in your lifetime. You have shrapnel embedded in your left trapezius and right buttock. I also noticed while operating that this is not your first gunshot wound. Perhaps it's time for you to find another line of work."

"I've been thinking about going to medical school. Then I could treat myself when I get shot."

She gave me a polite smile. "I had to sew the muscle in your thigh back together. I think we got all the shotgun pellets out, but we'll take another x-ray later to be sure. In any case, you are going to be off your feet for some time. Then you'll need to wear a special cast to keep it immobile for awhile. Do you have any questions?"

"When is my sponge bath?" I asked, trying to be cute. It was a distraction from my growing depression.

"The nurse on duty will be by later to give it to you. His name is John. He's very nice and will take good care of you," she said, her face serious.

The cop sitting next to my bed started to laugh.

"Any possibility of me getting a Jenny or Jessica, instead of John?"

"Sorry. John is the only nurse available."

I started to protest further, but stopped when I saw her chuckling.

"I'm just kidding. Your real nurse's name is Beth, and she'll give you one tomorrow. Just between you and me, the word around the ward is that she's looking forward to it." She gave me a wicked smile, slid my chart into its slot at the end of the bed, and walked out.

Later, the guy in the next bed lifted his oxygen mask and asked, "Those cigarettes next to your bed. They yours?"

"Yeah."

"I'm here cause I'm dying of lung cancer, and I'm only fifty-three. I suggest you quit. Those things are more dangerous than the shotgun that got you." His tone was kind and matter-of-fact, without the harping nagging quality that you usually hear from your average health Nazi. I was inclined to listen.

"Thanks. Maybe I'll do that."

"Hey, if you're quitting, give me the pack," said the cop, looking up from a wrinkled edition of *Ladies Home Journal*.

I hesitated, then grabbed the pack, and tossed it to him.

He made a good catch with one hand and said, "Thanks, I just ran out."

J.D. Miller

"Sure. Toss me that *Cosmo* you were looking at." Anything to keep my mind distracted from the searing, flashbulb memories of spurting blood, exploding heads, and the like. I knew from experience that they were sure to come. The possibility of dying didn't bother me. The killing did. It was as if every time I killed someone, I lost a little piece of my soul that I could never get back.

I was well into an fascinating article on "Getting Him To Commit: Ten Sure-fire Techniques," when Butch DeCarlo came in. He was thick-necked, barrel chested, and had a spade shaped jaw. The oxford shirt and tie he was wearing seemed misplaced on him. He looked like he should be wearing boxing trunks.

"What's with the *Cosmo*?" he asked.

"Hey, lay off my *Cosmo*. There are some good articles in here."

"How are you, buddy," he said, leaning over to give me a hug. "Good to see you're ok."

"Yeah, it was pretty close this time."

"Bad as Mogadishu?" he asked.

"No, not that bad."

"Well, I want you to know that we're going to pursue this further. You snipped off a couple of branches; now we're going for the roots.

"This all turned out to be much bigger than I expected."

"Yes, it did. You pried the lid off a whole lot of dirty shit that spreads world-wide."

"What about this Red Shield?" I asked. "Do I need to keep an eye out? Will they come after me?"

"I imagine they're annoyed at you for cutting off their supply of passports. But now that it's done, I suspect they'll just move on. To hit you after the deed is done will bring more heat than they need right now. Besides, they have a hundred other ways to get drugs in the country that don't require passports. They haven't been seriously crippled or threatened in any way. Better be careful for awhile though, just to be safe. These drug scum sometimes make emotional decisions, in which case they could very well act against their own best interests and try to take you out."

I ended up staying in the hospital another three days. Lillian Jones visited on the first day and spent a good four hours. She wanted to know everything, so I told her about the investigation in great detail, including the most important piece: that the man who had pulled the trigger in her son's murder was dead, along with one of his accomplices and the guy who planned it. The other accomplice would probably spend the better part of twenty years in jail.

Now that it was over, Ms. Jones finally allowed a volcano of suppressed emotions to erupt and had cried and sobbed and raged. Finally, she had released what she could and thanked me profusely for my services. She offered to help me when I got home with any housework or shopping until my leg healed. I gratefully accepted.

Greg and Aislinn visited daily. They were a joy to see, but the distance in Aislinn's eyes remained, and I continued to fear that we were finished.

Less joyous to see were the FBI, DEA, and IAD, who spent countless boring hours in my room, recording my statements. The IAD guy seemed bored and listless himself, and I doubted he would spend many hours trying to find the cops who drove Fredericks to the airport. I got the sense that he'd do enough to keep his superiors off his back, and that was it. In fairness to him, though, my descriptions hadn't given him much to work with. One black, one white, both mid-thirties and a bit thick around the middle. Probably described half the District PD.

My nurse Beth gave me a sponge bath, letting slip twice that she and her boyfriend of three years had just split up. Aislinn and I were still together, though, even if we were not likely to last, so I let the invitation pass. The sponge bath wasn't much fun, anyways. My leg had swollen to twice its normal size and hurt so badly that the doctor had upped my morphine. As a result, I was so doped up that I couldn't feel the sponge as she ran it over me. I had the strange impression throughout of watching a movie of someone giving me a bath. Visuals, but no corresponding sensations.

Finally, on my last day in the hospital, the dreams and flashbacks started, muted by the morphine pumping through my system. In one dream I was in a boat on a river, somewhere in Southeast Asia. The banks are lined with peasant huts, perched awkwardly next to the slow brown water of the river. Cargo nets hang everywhere from branches, poles, and roofs. Inside were the dead, some without arms, some without legs, young adults mostly, some children. Thousands of them hanging limply, decaying horribly. Strips of rotting flesh hung through the netting. It was a city of the dead. A young woman is my guide; she is alone in the city. She said, "Someday I hope to bury them all in huts, with dignity." The boat floats further downstream, and I am in a city much like Venice, the people laughing and dining, preparing to celebrate the New Year, oblivious to the horror upstream. I woke up shaking, feeling very alone.

- 20 -

It was a miserably hot, early summer day when Lillian Jones drove me home from the hospital; 97 degrees and 95 percent humidity. Typical Washington D.C. summer weather. It was one of those sticky, hot days where you could feel the bounds of self-restraint slip, and irritations and impatience sharply flare, the kind of heat that feeds the worst in people, sloth, hedonism, hatred.

The air-conditioner was out in Lillian's car, and despite the wind coming in through the window, my shirt was soon soaked with sweat. She looked perfectly comfortable, however, as we made our way out of the city and onto the highways leading to the Shenandoah.

"The heat don't bother me," she said. "It's the cold that's tough."

"I hate the heat."

"Eric was the same way. Used to sweat and sweat and bitch all summer," Lillian said. She smiled and then a shadow crossed her face. She lapsed into a depressed silence for a long time, then said, "I want to thank you again for what you've done. I wasn't quite sure what to make of you in the beginning, but you sure turned out to be all right."

"Well, I'm glad I was finally able to find the guys who did it. It's was touch-and-go there for quite awhile."

"You stuck with it, and the Lord finally showed you the way. God'll give you anything you want, but first he wants you to do the leg work, to show him that you *really* want it by sticking it out through the tough times."

"You really believe that?" I asked.

"Yes, I do. Think about it. Have you ever given you're all to something and not had it work out? You may not get *exactly* what you wanted, but you'll get something real close. As long as you don't half-step it."

"You've got a point," I admitted.

We drove in silence after that. Somewhere around Manassas, I fell asleep, drowsy from my latest dose of Percocet. She woke me up around Sperryville, asking for directions to my house. As we drove, I looked around at the magnificent mountains and rolling green hills and felt my soul settle in a nice way. Home again.

Lillian dropped me off in front of my house and offered to stay and help me get settled in. I thanked her, but refused. I just wanted to go inside and sleep some more. We agreed to get together for dinner sometime in the near future, and then she was gone, her car leaving a cloud of dust in it's wake as it backed down the mountain. I took in the view for a minute and then went toward the house, hobbling forward on my new crutches.

I opened the front door and looked down the barrel of a .38 Smith and Wesson.

"Come in, Mr. Christian," Phillip Riley said.

I did.

"Sit down," he said, motioning towards the chair wedged against the front wall.

I put my crutches down and eased into the chair.

"Welcome home," he said with absurd politeness. His voice was strained, and there were red blotches on his face. The gun shook slightly in his hand as he moved to my left and pressed the barrel against my temple.

"I should have figured this," I said. "Only someone in management could have altered the inventories."

"That's right. Do you think an idiot like Fredericks could have dealt with the paper trail? Do you know how many safeguards are in place to keep passports from being stolen?"

I didn't respond.

The hand holding the .38 shifted slightly, pressing the cold steel of the barrel more firmly into my left temple.

It's amazing the clarity of perception you get at moments like this. As the gun moved I could feel the curved striations of the inner barrel slightly scratching against my temple and the smooth expanse of it's outer surface, warming rapidly as it took the heat from my flesh. It was almost as if it was already drawing the life from me. I could hear the soft song of a bird perched outside the window, the low hum of the air conditioner, and the soft rythmic panting of Rachel, the world's *worst* watchdog. If I made it through this, I'd have to give her a class in doggy basics. Rule One: When someone is holding a gun to your masters head, *attack*. Don't lie under the kitchen table, watching the proceedings curiously.

So this is it, I thought, disappointed that my life was not flashing before my eyes. It would have probably been pretty interesting. I'd especially like to relive that night with Susie Johnson when I was 17. That was amazing. The things that girl could do with her... well, never mind... if I was going to heaven soon, thoughts of sex probably wouldn't help with my chances for admission. Better think something profound: recite the twenty-third psalm or something.

I'm surprised that I'm not feeling more panicked about all this. Don't get me wrong, I'm concerned, but not on the level one would expect. Maybe it has something to do with the large dose of Percocet I took in the car on the way here. It was muting the adrenaline dump that I usually got in these situations and making my instincts conspicuously absent. Where was that little voice that guided me unerringly in situations like this?

I tried to think it out, my mind sluggish. I had my .45 tucked into the waistband of my pants, in the back. Not a good place for a fast draw, especially when you're sitting down. I probably couldn't beat him to the trigger, but I promised myself that I would take him with me. All I had to do was get one shot off. The second that it looked like he was getting ready to fire, I would make my move, and try to knock his hand away, and draw my gun. It wasn't a great plan, but it was the best I could think of for now.

To distract him from pulling the trigger immediately, I started firing questions.

"Why did you do it? Fredericks, I can figure; he needed the money for drugs. But you! Why!?"

"I was doing the Lord's work," he said. I looked at his face, thinking that he must be joking. But his face was dead serious.

"How exactly is providing passports to major Asian drug dealers doing the Lord's work?"

"You've seen them; all those niggers and spics I work with," he said in a furious rush, the red in his face heightening, his knuckles white on the gun. "All of them are on drugs and fornicating and adultering and ruining everything for the rest of us so that a decent white people can't walk the streets in safety. And the government protects them! Gives them money and jobs that decent white folk could use. Let's them out of jail at the slightest excuse so they can run the streets. Hell, they kill each other all the time. Even they know how worthless they are!"

"So you provide passports to major drug dealers, to help them bring drugs into the country? Then you become an accessory to the murder of a man—a black man—who did nothing his whole life but go to church and try to help his community!?"

"In any war there is collateral damage," he said with absolute conviction. "When Eric came to me with his suspicions about missing passports, I tried to convince him to let it go. I told him that I had already looked into it, and there was nothing to it. But he was stubborn. He wouldn't stop investigating. He gave us no choice."

"You always have a choice. *Always*," I responded.

"Like I said, he was collateral damage. And providing sinners with the means of their destruction is no sin. It is God's justice at work."

"Is that what you see yourself doing?" I asked, amazed. "Helping drugs come into the country so that all the people you hate will destroy themselves? And God's Justice? Last time I read the Bible, there was a lot of talk about loving kindness and forgiveness and charity. I guess I missed the passages on drug dealing and genocide."

"You misunderstand the Bible then. 'I have pursued mine enemies, and destroyed them; and turned not again until I had consumed them.' That's Second Samuel 22, verse 38." In verse 41 it says 'Thou hast also given me the necks of mine enemies, that I might destroy them that hate me." In Psalm 139, verse 22 it commands us to 'hate them with a perfect hatred: I count them mine enemies." Riley looked at me triumphantly, impressed with his own ability to marshal an argument.

I started to respond by reminding him of the passages concerning 'love thy neighbor as thyself' and 'judge not lest ye be judged,' and 'take the log out of your own eye before taking the speck out of another's,' but before I could, there was a sharp knock at the door, and I heard Alicia Hunsaker call out, "Mark are you home?!"

Riley started in surprise and his eyes shifted to the door.

In that instant, I knocked his hand away from my head, drew my .45 and shot him in the right shoulder. He fired as a final reflex, but the shot went into the ceiling as he pitched over backwards.

Alicia screamed, and I could hear her footsteps as she ran away. Good. The sound of the gunshots had scared her away. I didn't want her to see this.

I got up and stood over Riley, the adrenaline firing through my system, oblivious of the need for crutches and the pain in my leg. It was an ugly scene. The round had gone through his shoulder, and blood was splattered on the back wall, looking like some abstract art from hell. Riley was on his back, already unconscious from shock, a pool of blood spreading rapidly in a circle around him. I thought about how

Riley had lived his life in hatred and bitterness and said to the now empty room, "What a wasted life."

-21-

The first couple of days after the shooting were spent in interviews with the local police, answering more endless questions.

Riley was taken to the hospital in Warrenton in critical, but stable, condition and kept under twenty-four-hour guard.

I spent some time in the city, staying with Greg in the priests quarters of his parish, trying to forget.

Now, back home, I sit in the carpet of wildflowers bordering the edge of my property, gazing down into the valley. It was the extremes that were helping me escape the ghosts that crowded my mind, threatening the sanity I so carefully constructed and maintained. Visions of the dead; shot, mutilated, limbs missing, bellies spilling open, brains blown out, staring at me with blaming eyes.

At night, in dreams, all the men I've killed come back to stand in judgment. One night they told me, "We are waiting for you," and I shot awake as I do most nights, sleepless till dawn. Down exhausted through the early morning, the only time when the ghosts recede and let me be.

I pursue intense experience relentlessly, anything to blowtorch my mind clean, to remove the space where insanity grows. Cornering on a country road at 80mph, knee barely brushing the road as I lean into the turn, inches from death. Massive muscle searing workouts, blasting back whiskey, parachuting with a local club, making love to Aislinn.

I think often about Phillip Riley and how he represents the worst in human nature: our ability to convince ourselves of anything and rationalize hurting others in the name of those beliefs, whether they be religious, racial, or political. The most destructive, dangerous people are those fanatics who have no doubt about the absolute rightness of their cause and are totally convinced of their right to impose it on others.

My thoughts are interrupted by a car coming up the mountain. It's a dingy, old light-blue Honda. It stopped in front of my house and Timmy Valentine got out and walked toward me.

He started to say *hi*, but froze before he could get it out, his gaze drawn out into the distance, lost in the view. He was *gone* for a long time, creating a silence that would have been uncomfortable with most people, but was not with him.

"God, it's incredible up here," he said finally.

"It sure is."

There was another stretch of silence while he sat down in the grass, took in an appreciative lungful of the clean air, and pondered the view. If he got this lost in everything that interested him, he was probably very good at whatever he did. Absolute immersion always creates excellence.

After a decent interval, I asked, "So, what brings you here?

"I wanted to tell you what I've found out about your unexpected visitor, Mr. Riley."

"Why not just call?" I asked.

"I did. You never answer your phone."

"True. I haven't wanted to lately."

"Anyway, I've always wanted to come out here on a weekend and thought I'd stop by on my way to Skyline Drive and see if I could catch you at home." His eyes followed the flight of a pair of butterflies, as they danced in air around us. He smiled in wonder and said, "*I taste a liquor never brewed...*"

"From tankards scooped in pearl. Inebriate of air am I and debauchee of dew," I continued for him.

"You missed a couple of lines, but that's pretty good. Not too many guys like you can quote Dickinson," he observed.

"Guys like me?" I asked smiling.

"Yeah. You know. Big muscle-bound, bruiser types."

It was said with wry humor, without the resentment that smaller men sometimes have for bigger ones, so I laughed, unoffended. Then I said, "I know I missed a couple of lines. I skipped them on purpose, cause they're my least favorite lines of the poem."

"Hmm," he mumbled as he pulled a small tattered notebook out of his back pocket. He flipped it open and said, "I've been investigating Phillip Riley, as a part of the FBI investigation into the theft of passports at the US Government Printing Office."

He paused, looking for the right place in his notes, then began reading. "Mr. Riley is a member of the Round Hill chapter of the Christian Identity, a white supremacist hate group that believes that Jews are biologically descended from Satan and that other minorities are 'soulless mud people' little different from animals.

"His chapter is one of the more extreme ones, as compared to those that advocate for separation. They want elimination, saying that Christ will not return to earth until it is wiped clean of Jews and minorities. Also to be eliminated are any other 'Satanic influences,' meaning white people who do not support their cause. Included in that is the US government. Last week, as a result of my and your investigations, FBI and ATF agents raided the Christian Identity complex in Round Hill and found over fifty fully automatic weapons and a variety of homemade bombs, some of which could easily bring down a building. Most of the members have been found and are in custody, charged with an assortment of felonies."

He paused to take a breath and then continued. "Mr. Riley is a leader of the group and considered an 'expert' in Biblical interpretation. He frequently posted essays on their website, using only his first name. The essays were long rants, heavy on interpretations of scripture that rationalized Christian Identity beliefs and tactics. At the time of his death, he had over $400,000 in four different bank accounts, which I traced backwards to money laundered through various banks in Singapore. Despite the money, Mr. Riley spent frugally, spending little more than his salary in the last fiscal year. His credit rating was perfect, and he had no credit card debt. He saw his doctor three times in the last year for stress-related complaints. He prescribed Ativan once, but never filled the prescription. Oh, yeah, I almost forgot...the money in his accounts were frozen yesterday by the U.S. Government."

"You found all that out on the computer?" I asked, fairly amazed.

"Yep. With the internet, if you have the skills, you can find out just about anything about anyone."

"How do you like the FBI?" I asked.

"I like the work I do, but I don't fit in. I don't like bureaucracy and don't deal well with authority. They're always giving me a hard time about my appearance. The only reason they haven't fired me is because they don't have many people who can do what I do."

"Ever thought about becoming a private investigator? Computers are the tool of the future in my job, and you don't have a boss or a dress code."

He looked at me for a second, then said, "Are you offering me a job?"

"I tend to make intuitive decisions, and I've got a good feeling about you. I'm thinking an apprenticeship, leading to a partnership. I'll train you in the beginning, and then eventually we can work our own cases and help each other as needed. We have some very different, but complementary, skills that I think will work well together. The downside is a lot of long boring stretches tailing people, no retirement plan or medical benefits, and times where the money is tight."

"What about the danger?" he asked.

"I don't consider that a downside."

"Well, I do."

"That's ok. I'll handle that end of things as much as possible. With the exception of taking shifts helping me tail people, you'll mostly do what you're doing now; find stuff out about people and companies on the computer."

He looked out over the valley again. "Is your office out here?"

"It's in Old Town Warrenton, a beautiful town about a half hour east of here. If you needed a place to stay, you could crash in my house until you find something. That's, of course, assuming what happened in there doesn't freak you out."

"You mean Riley getting shot?"

"Yeah."

"As long as you cleaned up, I don't care." Then he paused and took another long look out over the valley. Finally he turned to me and smiled and said, "I'll give my notice on Monday."

THE END

ABOUT THE AUTHOR

J.D. Miller, MA, CPP-G, MAC is a certified professional counselor and award-winning writer. He has been published in several professional journals and made numerous TV appearances. This novel draws primarily on his experiences working as a substance abuse counselor, treating heroin and crack addicts in the most violent, impoverished neighborhoods in Washington, D.C. He currently lives in Warrenton, Virginia with his wife, son, and two dogs.